W9-BVX-943

DISCARD

Also by Wesley King

The Incredible Space Raiders from Space!

OCDaniel

A World Below

sara
and the
search
for
normal

WESLEY KING

A Paula Wiseman Book · Simon & Schuster Books for Young Readers · NEW YORK LONDON TORONTO SYDNEY NEW DELHI

SIMON & SCHUSTER BOOKS FOR YOUNG READERS
An imprint of Simon & Schuster Children's Publishing Division
1230 Avenue of the Americas, New York, New York 10020

This book is a work of fiction. Any references to historical events,
real people, or real places are used fictitiously. Other names, characters, places,
and events are products of the author's imagination, and any resemblance to actual
events or places or persons, living or dead, is entirely coincidental.
Text copyright © 2020 by Wesley King
Jacket illustration copyright © 2020 by Elizabeth Casal
All rights reserved, including the right of reproduction in whole or in part in any form.

SIMON & SCHUSTER BOOKS FOR YOUNG READERS
is a trademark of Simon & Schuster, Inc.
For information about special discounts for bulk purchases, please contact
Simon & Schuster Special Sales at 1-866-506-1949 or business@simonandschuster.com.
The Simon & Schuster Speakers Bureau can bring authors to your live event.
For more information or to book an event, contact the Simon & Schuster Speakers Bureau
at 1-866-248-3049 or visit our website at www.simonspeakers.com.
Book design by Tom Daly
The text for this book was set in Adobe Garamond Pro.
Manufactured in the United States of America
0320 FFG
First Edition
2 4 6 8 10 9 7 5 3 1
Library of Congress Cataloging-in-Publication Data
Names: King, Wesley, author.
Title: Sara and the search for normal / Wesley King.
Description: First edition. | New York : Simon & Schuster Books for Young Readers, [2020] | "A
Paula Wiseman Book." | Audience: Ages 8-12. | Audience: Grades 4-6. | Summary: Seventh-grader
Sara wants to be normal but her panic attacks and other episodes cause her to isolate herself until, in
group therapy, she meets talkative and outgoing Erin, her first friend.
Identifiers: LCCN 2019028307 (print) | LCCN 2019028308 (eBook)
ISBN 9781534421134 (hardback) | ISBN 9781534421158 (eBook)
Subjects: CYAC: Friendship—Fiction. | Mentally ill—Fiction. | Panic attacks—Fiction.
Behavior—Fiction. | Family problems—Fiction.
Classification: LCC PZ7.K58922 Sar 2020 (print) | LCC PZ7.K58922 (eBook)
DDC [Fic]—dc23
LC record available at https://lccn.loc.gov/2019028307

For the Star Kids

R0457317410

INTRODUCTION

THE BEGINNING OF THE STORY OF THE END OF SARA MALVERN

Introductions are hard, so let's just start by punching something.

I was six years old, but I remember that day perfectly. Especially the lavender. The smell of lavender used to remind me of toilets. Now it reminds me of blood.

My mom was taking me dress shopping for her cousin Bethany's wedding. That sounds nice, except I didn't like shopping, or busy places, or dresses. I didn't like lots of things. Still don't. Mom always told me I was a "problematic child," but I was about to give her some fancy new labels to use.

My dad walked into my room the night before and sat down on my bed.

"Sara, try hard for me tomorrow," he said. "Okay?"

I used to sleep like a vampire, so I was staring at the ceiling with my arms folded across my chest. It was a simple precaution: No self-respecting vampire would prey on one of their own.

"Okay," I said.

"Promise that you'll try your best to behave yourself. This means a lot to your mother."

"I promise."

Stupid Sara. Promises always cause problems.

The next day my mom combed my hair and put a navy blue bow in it and took a picture. I didn't complain once on the drive, even though she talked the whole time about how a green dress would match my dark eyes. She kept talking all the way to a store called Elleries'. The windows were full of poof-y dresses, and remember, everything smelled like a toilet. Mom took my hand and led me to the counter.

"We have an appointment for a dress for my daughter," she said proudly.

A lady with white hair looked over the counter. "What a dear! I have some set aside."

Before I knew it, I was in a dressing room with five dresses and a mirror. I could hear my mom talking with the saleslady. Her name was Anne and she was the living epicenter of the lavender. She wanted to help me change, but my mom said, "It's okay, she is a big girl, she can do it." I do enjoy a vote of confidence, but really she just knew I would scream if Anne touched me.

I put on the red dress and stepped out, eyes on the floor.

They cooed and clucked and wanted to see another one. I didn't like being stared at—another one of the many things I don't like—but I went back inside to change anyway.

"You made a promise," I reminded the impatient girl in the mirror.

There was pink. Then blue. I put on a green one and tried to stay calm. I was starting to feel warm and more strangers were looking when I came out and I could hear my mom talking.

"This is very good for her," she whispered. "She has . . . some challenges with new things."

"She seems lovely," Anne said.

I rubbed my forehead because it seemed like everything was getting louder. It did that sometimes. Voices bounced around my head, or maybe my brain just said them back to me like an echo in a cavern.

She. She. *She*. My name is Sara Malvern, toilet lady. I am not lovely when I scream.

"Thank you for saying that," my mom said. "It can be difficult."

"Is she . . . ill?" Anne asked.

They were still whispering, but quiet people are experts at listening.

"No, no. Some behavioral things. It's hard with strangers."

"Oh. She's very shy, for sure," Anne said. "Not a peep out of her this whole time."

My mom laughed. "You have no idea."

I tried to calm down. The voices were still ricocheting around and the dressing room felt smaller now. The green dress was pooling on the floor like a moat and I was drowning in it. I was wondering why I had behavioral things and why Mom made me come here if I was so *difficult*. The thoughts flowed one into another until they became a flood.

I hate dresses. I hate strangers.

But as I stood there looking at myself in the mirror, afraid, I realized:

I hate Sara Malvern most.

"I'm finished," I said loudly.

"Well, let's see it, then," my mom replied.

"I want to leave now."

There was a long silence.

"There's only two more dresses," she said.

The room is shrinking I am so hot I can't breathe I can't breathe. I tried not to scream.

"Can we leave?" I asked again in my most polite I-am-losing-my-temper voice.

"Just try the blue one."

It turns out that when I am panicking, I do not compromise well.

But I wasn't really mad at them. I was mad at the girl in the mirror.

I slammed my fist into the mirror and maybe I had pointy

knuckles or maybe it was a cheap mirror because it shattered. I screamed as my knuckles bled. I shrunk down into the corner and started crying because I had made such a mess, and I didn't know if I had punched the mirror or the girl in it. Mostly I knew that I was not normal and if there had ever been a normal girl in the mirror, she was in a thousand pieces now.

I had locked the dressing-room door even though they said not to, but Anne had a key and they found me bleeding. Anne gasped and my mother cried. Mom used her credit card to pay for the mirror. Anne brought paper towels and Band-Aids. Mom put them on and cried while she did it. We didn't speak in the car. When we got home, my mom went to her room and she didn't come out again until dinner. My dad came into my room later that day.

"You promised me, Sara," he said, looking over my bandaged hands.

He was disappointed and that hurt worse than glass.

The next day my parents took me to a child psychiatrist. I guess technically he was the one who gave them those fancy new labels. He wasn't shy about handing them out either.

After a few sessions I had all kinds of them:

1. Bipolar Disorder: dramatic mood swings, emotional instability
2. General Anxiety Disorder: difficulty relaxing, panic attacks, trouble breathing

3. Mild Schizophrenia: distorted reality, paranoia
4. Depression: a constant sense of dread, unshakable sadness

He gave me my first pills and now I take four every day. I also realized something after the punch, besides the fact that green was not my color. Sometimes I hear people say, "It must be hard to be crazy." And it is. But they should also say, "It must be hard to love someone who is crazy." They have to see the pain, but they never hear the whispers.

Oh, I'm sorry. I told you introductions were hard. Let's start again.

My name is Sara Malvern and it's very nice to meet you.

CHAPTER 1

MY HAPPY FAMILY

Five years after breaking the mirror, I was sitting on the stairs like a gargoyle. I do that a lot. I hunch forward with my arms around my legs, and even though I don't have wings, I lean precariously far over the steps.

"—you have to admit that it isn't working."

That's my mom. She is still embarrassed that she has a crazy daughter.

"She's fine, Michelle."

That's my dad. He loves me.

"Fine? Her teacher said she panicked today and wouldn't eat—"

"It can be stressful at school—"

"It's normal to be in school," she cut in sharply. "She's in seventh grade. This is not normal."

"Keep your voice down."

"I just . . . I'm worried."

She worried a lot.

"What do you want to do? She's on the medication. She goes to therapy."

"It's not enough."

My dad laughed, but not in a nice way. "So, what? More drugs?"

"Maybe. Or . . . you know what Dr. Ring said."

"You want to send her away."

"It's a six-month program. Maybe a year. She needs intensive—"

"You want to put her in a padded room. My little girl."

"*Our* little girl—" my mom said.

"No, you've obviously decided she isn't yours anymore."

"How dare you say that to me. After all I have been through."

"And Sara and I are so sorry you've had to *suffer*."

The silence made my head hurt.

"I can't do this with you," my mom said. "I can't."

"So don't," he replied. "Let me worry about Sara."

"Sara is sick, and you won't even admit it."

"We are all sick, Michelle. We just have different diseases."

My mother stormed off, my father slammed a door, and the gargoyle brooded. I am the gargoyle, in case you forgot. I went to bed after a while. I tried to sleep, but I am good at thinking and bad at sleeping. I gave up and wandered downstairs. Mom had gone to bed, but Dad was usually up late. He was a municipal waste specialist and woke up very early, but he always had a nap when he got home and then had trouble sleeping later. The TV was on.

I walked down the hall in silence. Sneaking was easy in my house. We had shag carpet the color of skin that my dad said was "perfectly serviceable," though my mom kept accidentally spilling red wine on it.

I found Dad in the living room. He was asleep. There were empty beer bottles on the carpet and his hand was curled up beside them like a dead spider.

"Oh, Daddy," I said, sighing.

I threw a blanket over him, grabbed his phone, and set an alarm for four thirty a.m. My dad looked younger when he was asleep. He was somewhere else now. I hoped it was a happy place.

I sat down next to him and watched a whole documentary about blue whales. I love whales and everything in the sea. The whales were gathered near Hawaii and singing beautifully. The narrator said they usually swim alone, but that sometimes they get together and hang out.

"We don't know what they're saying," I said as my dad snored, "but I bet it's something very wise. Maybe they are saying, 'It would be nice to swim together forever. But we all must be going. You see, we must swim alone. We are too big.

It has been lovely to have some friends, even if it was only for a little while.'"

I fell asleep on his legs and woke up the next morning tucked into my bed.

NOTE

If you ask a blue whale what she thinks about—if you sing whale, of course—you might be surprised. Most people would guess it was about krill, or ocean currents, or maybe if she was due for some air. But it could also be about her baby who swam off two years ago and whether he found a girlfriend. Or that dolphins are silly. Or maybe that the stars look beautiful tonight, even from underwater. We can't ask her, so we all just kind of assume it's the krill.

Do me a favor, even if it is just for this story: Assume it's the stars.

CHAPTER 2

TALKATIVE TUESDAYS

The next day I was sitting in class. Well, my class. It's a yellow room with some ugly artwork and motivational posters plastered on the wall that say things like YOU ARE A STAR! and HANG IN THERE! That one had a kitten hanging onto a power line. It probably should have said ANIMAL CRUELTY SELLS POSTERS! I call my class the Crazy Box, but Ms. Hugger doesn't like that name.

"Sara, are you paying attention?" Ms. Hugger asked.

Ms. Hugger liked me sometimes. She had a boyfriend named Sven and she was going for the all-time teaching record of one year with Sara Malvern. There should have been a plaque.

I looked up from my notebook. "Partially."

I only talk to four people: my mom sometimes, my dad always, Ms. Hugger sometimes, and my current psychiatrist,

Dr. Ring, on Tuesday nights. I hadn't talked to *anyone* else for three years, six months, and eleven days. It was a Tuesday, so it was going to be a very talkative day.

"Can I have your full attention?"

I considered that. I was drawing a picture of myself standing on the bridge of the *Starship Enterprise*, which probably wasn't critical.

"Yes," I said, putting my pen down.

"Thank you." She turned back to the board. "Now, if you carry the six—"

"Can I put my head down?"

Sometimes I do that during the day. I don't sleep or anything. Not usually. I just let the world go quiet.

"We're almost done—" she said.

"The answer is forty-six," I murmured, making a nest with my arms.

I heard her drawing out the problem and mouthing out the answers as I put my head down. Then she sighed and sat down at her desk. She doesn't like when I jump ahead of her, but I do it a lot. My brain solves things easily. It remembers everything. Well, except how to behave.

"What are you thinking about?" Ms. Hugger asked.

I tried to pick out one thing. "That it would be nice to be in normal class sometimes."

She was quiet for a moment. "We can try that again one day—"

"No," I said. "Strike that. It would be nice to be a normal student sometimes."

Ms. Hugger walked over with a pillow. She always has one ready.

"In ten minutes we should get back to work."

"Okay."

She crouched down next to me and spoke softly. "Are you about to start a Game?"

I had my eyes open, but they were full of sweater. "I don't know. Maybe."

"Which one?"

I thought about that. I could feel the tightness in my chest, like a bubble being blown up and stretching out just below my lungs, pushing everything out . . . the air and the calm and Sara.

"False Alarm, I think," I whispered.

It was the Game that meant panic attack.

"What do you call a fish without an eye?" she asked, squeezing my arm.

I tried to think. "What?"

"*Fsh.*"

I smiled into my sweater. She gave me a pat on the back and went to her desk. I had avoided a panic attack, and that was nice. But I wasn't stupid. Normal kids didn't have to put their heads down in class. They didn't need Ms. Hugger to tell them jokes. And so I hugged the pillow and rocked back and forth for a little while, letting my hair fall over my eyes like someone had pulled the curtains shut. The other kids in school had a name for me. *Psycho Sara.*

They weren't wrong.

A boy sat down across from me. He was new to Dr. Ring's office.

His black hair was curly and sprinkled with blond highlights that had almost grown out. His skin was dark, even darker under his eyes. It looked like he had been crying recently. He glanced up at me, and I turned back to my magazine. Dr. Ring said I shouldn't stare at people. It makes them uncomfortable. But the boy turned back to his cell phone, so I snuck another look.

I decided he was about twelve. He was wearing black Nike shorts, white sneakers, and a faded plaid button-down. He was alone, which was no surprise. Dr. Ring liked parents to drop us off at the door so that the kids "took ownership of their therapy" and didn't feel like we were trapped here, even though we were. My mom was in the car doing a crossword puzzle and would pounce on me if I made a break for it. I know because it happened one time.

Dr. Ring appeared at the door to his office. He was tall and thin and pinkish-pale, with a few wispy tufts of white hair that liked to stand up. I guess the whole thing was technically his office; a glass door from outside led to a small lobby with dark green walls like a forest and then two more doors—one to the therapy room and the other to a bathroom. There was also a desk for a receptionist, but Dr. Ring never seemed to hire one, so it was usually just me and some fake ferns hanging out until he was ready for the appointment. And now this new boy, apparently.

"Come in, James," Dr. Ring said. "Sara, we are just going to have a quick chat. I will be with you soon."

Then he disappeared back into his office.

James stood up and went to join him. He looked at me and smiled.

"Hey, Sara."

James closed the door behind him, and I sat there, frowning.

I picked up a magazine and read about developments in brain science. None of it seemed like it was going to fix me.

They were in there for twenty-two minutes. There is a clock on the wall that alternates between silence and the loudest noise in the world, depending on your level of attention. Then James walked out and smiled at me again. I looked away because he was a stranger and therefore not to be trusted. But the way he stared at me made my skin tingle. I was glad he left.

"Sorry, Sara," Dr. Ring said. "Come on in."

I sat down on the red corduroy couch that was reserved for crazies, and Dr. Ring sat in the red corduroy chair beside it, which was reserved for him. He was nice enough. He liked clipboards and talking about the past, but I think that was his job description.

"What does he have?" I asked, looking toward the exit.

Dr. Ring raised his bushy white eyebrows. He did that a lot.

"You know I can't tell you that," Dr. Ring said.

His voice was low and sounded a little British. I know because I watch *Doctor Who*.

"I'll figure it out," I said.

He sighed. "I don't doubt it. Ms. Hugger told me you nearly had a panic attack today. Or what is it you call it?"

"False Alarm," I muttered.

They had set up a support network so Ms. Hugger could call my mom and dad and doctor and probably my friends if I had any. I imagined sometimes their faces popped up in holograms around a table and they said things like "the old evil has risen" or "there has been a disturbance."

"We might want to look at upping your medications to thirty milligrams. It would help."

"Why not sixty?" I said softly, staring at the dusty books behind him. The titles were *Talking Through Grief* and *Child Psychology* and *The Mysterious Brain*. Dr. Ring let me borrow them, and I had read every single one. None of those had fixed me either.

"Sara, you know the medications are helpful. You know what it was like before."

"I don't, actually."

"You were having a difficult time," Dr. Ring said. He was already writing something down. "I read all of the old reports. Daily panic attacks. Mood swings. Depression."

"Sounds familiar."

"It was much worse. You are too hard on yourself. You are much more stable now. Not as many wild swings. Fewer episodes. We are going to try to get them down to zero. I am going to sign off on the thirty milligrams of citalopram and thirty milligrams of lithium. It's an effective combination."

"And very normal."

Dr. Ring looked up from his notes. "Excuse me?"

I didn't meet his eyes. I just stared at the old books. It was all I liked about his office.

"Taking brain pills. It's very normal. Just like all the other kids at school."

"Sara, what did I tell you about your obsession with normal?"

I kept my eyes on the books. "To give up on it?" I whispered.

"To *redefine* the idea," he said. "What do I always tell you? What was the first thing I said when we started?"

I sighed. "If I want to be someone else at the end of this, then I will be disappointed."

"Exactly."

I ran a finger along the back of my hand. I felt it, but I

wondered if it felt the same for normal kids. Maybe they felt every pore. Every hair. It was hard to trust anything when you were crazy.

I stopped on my knuckles and remembered the blood. There were still a few little white scars like my mom's sunspots.

"I would also like to recommend you for group therapy," Dr. Ring said.

My eyes flicked back to him. "What?"

"You don't have to talk. But there are other kids like you. You can just listen to them."

I could already feel my throat drying up. I wanted to cough, but Dr. Ring would write it down. He said my coughing was a nervous tic, something called a *habit cough*, but it wasn't official yet, and I didn't want another label.

"That sounds like a bad idea," I said.

He smiled. "It will help. Being around other kids might be very cathartic for you. Even if you don't talk. Trust me. They are every Thursday night."

"I'm busy Thursdays."

"Are you really?" he asked skeptically.

I stink at lying. "I could be."

"And now you are. Let's talk about this near panic attack. Tell me how it started."

I stared at the books again for a moment. He always let the silence hold.

"I wish I knew," I said finally. "I must have done something very wrong."

I wasn't talking about today, and he knew that. He knew who I blamed for all of this.

And so he told me for the hundredth time it wasn't my fault that I was sick.

And for the hundredth time, I pretended to believe him.

NOTE (ABOUT GAMES)

Confused about the Games? Don't feel bad. I explained it to Dr. Ring, like, seven times. There are three different ones. In order of most common to least common:

1. False Alarm
2. The Lead Ball
3. The Danger Game

False Alarm is a fancy name for panic attacks. To be clear, they are *real* panic attacks, but the reason I get them is a total lie. Like, my brain tells me I am dying. Of course, I'm not. Not really. And every time when the panic attack is over, I realize it was another false alarm. You'd think I would be ready. But my brain is a wonderful actor and makes me think I am dying every single time. And she does that during breakfast, or when I'm on the toilet, or in class, or in bed, and even when I say, "Can we please do this later?" she makes me play anyway.

The Lead Ball. I got this name from *A Christmas Carol.* You know those ghosts with the lead balls and manacles? Well, sometimes it feels like I have chains strapped to me. But I still have to go to school, so I just grab the lead ball and drag it for as long as I can. I feel heavy almost all the time, but it gets worse some days. Much worse. Dr. Ring says it is the depressive symptoms.

The Danger Game is my term for schizophrenic episodes. I don't get them much, only when I am tired. Some people have them all the time. Instead of guessing if I am dying, I have to guess if *other* people are trying to hurt me. It's tricky, and I always think they are, and they never do.

Why all the names? I don't know. I guess I like the idea of them being a Game.

It means that someday, maybe, I might just win.

CHAPTER 3

WEDNESDAY IS WORSE

Ms. Hugger let me eat lunch in the cafeteria on Wednesday. I ask all the time, since that is where the normal kids eat, but we only do it twice a week. She says any more than that would be "putting a strain on" me. Crowds bring out the Danger Game, and that one never ends well.

But ironically, I like watching people. I think I even like people in general, most of the time. I just can't talk to them because we don't speak the same language. One of us has to learn.

I bit into my peanut butter and jelly and mayonnaise sandwich (salty, sweet, and tangy!) and watched as three girls walked by: Raya, Liz, and Ashley. They were the same age as me but popular and therefore not crazy on the outside. Ashley saw me watching them and made a face.

"Why do they let Psycho Sara in here? She's going to kill

us," she whispered except loud enough that I could hear. She had always been a terrible whisperer.

The other kids seemed to say that a lot—that I was dangerous and wanted to hurt them. The idea was a little insulting. Why would my brain want to hurt them? It was busy hurting me.

Ms. Hugger looked up from her cell phone and scowled. "I am going to report that girl."

"It's fine," I said.

"It's not fine."

Ms. Hugger's cell phone buzzed, and she glanced down, frowning.

"It's Sven. I have to step out and take this," she said. "You all right for a moment?"

I nodded and took another bite of my sandwich.

She hurried out, and I was suddenly alone in the busy cafeteria—a rare occurrence. Actually, I am almost never alone at school. It's strange, because I always feel lonely here.

I wasn't alone for long.

"Talk to her," a boy said, pushing his friend and laughing.

It was Taj. He was a football player—burly, athletic, and intentionally dim-witted, which is my least favorite type of personality. He was with Tom, who was all of those things but maybe nicer.

He was also best friends with my favorite people-watching target of all. More on that later.

"Leave it," Tom said.

"She likes you," Taj replied, winking at me. "Right, Psycho Sara?"

I told you they called me that. I guess it has an alliterative ring. Sometimes I call myself that name when I'm not thinking.

I felt my cheeks go warm. He gave Tom another push.

"C'mon, Tom's cute, isn't he?" Taj said, grabbing for Tom's arm.

Tom yanked it away, flushed crimson now, and Taj sighed.

"Fine, fine. I guess it would be an awkward date." He wandered over to my table and picked up my sandwich, looking it over. "At least you eat. You are a human, I think. Except . . . what is that white stuff? Is that *mayonnaise* with PB and J? Ugh. I take it back."

"Leave her alone, man," Tom said. "You're sick."

Taj laughed. "Just joking around. I know she's retarded."

He put the sandwich down, and I kept my eyes there. I hate that word. They call me that one a lot too. I hate the way it sounds. I hate what it means to them. That I am not like them because I am broken. Because I am most definitely *not* normal.

And now I also hated that I had mayonnaise on my sandwich because obviously that wasn't right, and I didn't know that. Now I wasn't hungry, and my stomach hurt. I stared at the sandwich, and I hated the girl that had wanted it because she wasn't right either.

I knew that, of course. I just liked to pretend some days. Just for lunch.

But I could not say those things to Taj. I couldn't say anything he would understand.

I am a blue whale, and my songs are only noise to anyone but me.

He hurried away just as Ms. Hugger returned.

"Did he say something to you?" she asked.

"Not really," I whispered, putting my lunch away. "Just called me a retard, is all."

"I'm so sorry, Sara," she said. "I will go talk to Principal Surrin—"

"Can we go back to our classroom now?"

"Yeah," she said softly. "Let's go."

She led me back to the Crazy Box, and my brain called me a retard the whole way there until I said, "Yes, I know I am. You don't have to rub it in."

Then Ms. Hugger closed the door behind us, and I sat down and tried not to cry and failed.

When I got home, I went to my room and took out my list. It's written on one of those big spiral notepads with lots of lined pages. The first page had a scribbled title:

Rules for Being Normal

I started it two years ago, and I had been adding to it ever since. I flipped through the pages. There were a lot of them. Some of the rules had been crossed off, which meant I had actually accomplished it, but not many. Not enough.

I went right to the end and added the newest entry.

137. Don't put mayonnaise on your peanut butter and jelly sandwiches.

Then I went to the beginning and started reading them slowly, to remember. I do that once a day. I knew that if I tried hard enough, if I spent every day reminding myself that I was not normal but maybe I could be, then I had a chance to get better. I could be Normal Sara. I didn't know what she was like. I don't even know if she ever existed, even before the broken mirror. But she had to be better than this.

"Fifty-seven. Talk to somebody your age. Fifty-eight. Try to make eye contact with a stranger. Fifty-nine. Don't go the bathroom to calm down for one entire day. Sixty. Try to be . . ."

We have pasta on Wednesday nights. Sometimes my mom would try rotini noodles or a thick Bolognese sauce, but my dad and I always complained. We liked plain noodles and plain sauce and routines. Dad sat on one end of the table, and Mom on the other. I sat between them.

"How was your day?" my mom asked my dad.

I looked at my dad. He was just shoveling his spaghetti down, eyes on the table.

"Fine."

She took a bite, chewing slowly. "Mine too. It's been busy at work."

Nobody said anything. I just ate my spaghetti. Dinner was always quiet lately.

My mom dabbed her face with a napkin. "Sara, are any of the kids . . . giving you trouble?"

I glanced at her warily. "No."

"Ms. Hugger emailed me something this evening."

My dad was watching me now too. "I didn't see this email."

"She mentioned an incident where another student might have said something."

"Ms. Hugger likes to exaggerate," I said.

"Kids can be rough sometimes," she said. "They don't understand . . . differences."

"What did they say?" my dad asked.

"Nothing," I replied.

His face was turning red now. "Did they call you names? Did they hurt you?"

He had put his fork down. One hand was squeezing the end of the table.

"It's nothing, Daddy."

I tried to grab his hand, but he pulled it away.

"Tell me!" he shouted.

I don't like when my father is angry. And I do not lie to him. Ever.

"He said I was a retard," I whispered. My hands came back to my lap to hide there.

"Who?" he said softly.

My mom could see what was coming now. "Let's just relax. We can talk later—"

"*Who?*" he demanded. He stood up so fast his chair fell over. "Tell me!"

I don't do well with shouting. I like the quiet, and shouting makes my brain shout too.

"I don't know!" I said, my hands over my ears. "I don't know!"

I didn't like Taj. But I didn't want anything to happen to him. My dad had threatened a boy for calling me a freak a few years ago, and he had almost been charged.

"Tell me!" he screamed.

"I don't know!"

One day Dr. Ring told me emotions were like a tide. They rise higher and higher and it is hard to stop them once they start. But normal people build walls and breakers. When the water comes, it doesn't destroy anything. I don't have those. And so when the tide comes, it washes me away.

Now my dad was screaming, "Tell me!" and threatening

to go to my school and saying terrible curse words, and my mom was trying to calm him down, and good-bye, Sara Malvern.

The water sprung out of my eyes and nose and I beat the table with my fists until my plate shattered on the floor and my brain said, "Retard, Retard, Retard!" and there was spaghetti everywhere and my mother was shouting and my father was raging and that was our Wednesday night dinner.

NOTE

Maybe you are wondering, "Do you really talk to your brain, Sara? That's weird because you are your brain." But the answer is yes, because my brain can be a bully, and sometimes it feels much better to say, "Back off, stupid brain!" than to say, "I don't like myself," even if they mean the same thing. If that confuses you, don't worry. That makes two of us.

CHAPTER 4

FLOWERS AND SAILBOATS

The next day I was home alone after school. Usually my dad is there having a nap, but for the last few months he has been late a lot. Mom yelled at him about it and he said he would try harder, but this was already the second day this week. It was fine. I was twelve now, and crazy or not, I could take care of myself. Sometimes I liked to be alone. Most of the time. Why?

1. It's normal to feel lonely when you are by yourself.
2. I could cough or pace or scream and it wouldn't bother anyone.
3. The only person that said mean things to me was me.

But today I was nervous. I had my first group session in a few hours. With other kids.

So, I used the afternoon to read *Harry Potter and the*

Sorcerer's Stone for the tenth time. I like it the best because I get to spend time with non-magic Harry when his life stinks and then discovers that he is actually special and his life is going to rule. It's just like me except I do have a bedroom and parents. No owl, though, so it's sort of a wash.

I read a lot. Reading is when my brain goes the most quiet. It doesn't call me anything or think about my day or make me play Games that I don't want to. Mom said it was fine to read all night, but that I had to take breaks. So every hour I get up and stretch or jump or do a little dance if my door and the curtains are closed. I have a laptop and a cell phone, but I am not allowed to have internet on them because of some previous incidents.

So I just put on the radio and dance to whatever is on.

I don't think I am very good. But I do love to dance. We have dances at school once in a while, and I always go. I don't dance, but I still watch, and dream, and make plans.

One day I will be better. Normal. I will have friends and I will dance. I just had to follow the rules. I had to talk. I had to get rid of the Games. I would be normal. I would.

"Do normal kids have to try to be normal?" my brain asked. That thought settled in. I don't know if most people feel their thoughts. Some of mine are light, and some of mine are heavy. And when the heavy ones come, they stay and spread out too.

Another Game. It was the Lead Ball, and my body got

heavy. I lay back in bed and opened my book and tried to go back to Hogwarts, where a spell could probably fix me.

Later that evening, at seven o'clock sharp, I found myself sitting on a stiff chair in a circle of kids.

There were four other kids there: three girls including me and one boy. Not James. I was a little disappointed, which didn't make any sense. Then again, my brain never makes sense.

"We are welcoming a new member today," Dr. Ring said. "Her name is Sara."

There were a few murmured hellos. I think one girl was having a panic attack.

Dr. Ring folded his hands and smiled.

"Sara, we don't do anything too formal. We just meet and talk about our weeks and any issues that might have popped up. Sometimes we discuss certain themes that I have prepared. It's all very conversational, just like our individual sessions. Everyone should feel comfortable. This is a nonjudgmental, safe space. Okay?"

Bad start there, but I nodded so everyone would stop looking at me.

Dr. Ring's office felt small when there were five people inside. It was all bouncing knees and watching eyes. A little ball formed in my throat. That is always a warning sign for False Alarm. It's like someone is pressing their fingers against my windpipe. I fought the urge to cough or fidget. I didn't want to embarrass myself on the first day.

"Great," Dr. Ring said, checking his clipboard. "Would anyone like to start? Mel?"

That was the panic attack girl, but she was busy trying to breathe. I watched as she tried to force it down, smiling with only the edge of her lips, and everyone just waited for her to start. That was different. Normally people laughed or looked uncomfortable or said something mean.

These kids just . . . waited.

I had never really been around other crazy people. There weren't any at my school—apart from one, maybe—and it was fascinating to watch anxiety or whatever Mel had work its way through her body. It was like looking in a mirror. Her feet shifted. Her fingers searched for something to hold. Mine started to do the same, and I wanted to chew my nails, but fought it down. The boy was already chewing his, and there wasn't much left of them. Why was I here?

Was I really as bad as them?

"What do you have?" someone whispered.

I turned and found a girl staring at me. She had wavy red-brown hair and a lot of freckles. She had almost no eyelashes—just a few stray ones at the corners of her eyes—and her eyebrows were nearly gone as well, except for some stubble.

She was still waiting for an answer. I shook my head.

"I don't get it," she said.

I shook my head again.

"You don't talk," she said, grinning. "That's so cool!"

That was news to me, but I nodded, hoping she would stop talking.

"I'm Erin," she said, sliding her chair a little closer. "You? Oh, right. The mutism. Never mind. Is that your problem?" She slapped her forehead. "Why do I keep asking? I am going to have to work on my sign language. And by that, I mean completely learn it from scratch. How long do you think it would take? Ugh, I did it again. What if I wrote notes instead? Or like a code . . . one blink yes, two blinks no, three blinks maybe . . . Hmm. Could be a lot of blinking—"

"Erin?" Dr. Ring said. "Would you like to share?"

Erin sat up and tapped her chair thoughtfully. "Well, it was a pretty good week, I guess."

"Why is that?" Dr. Ring asked.

"She still has eyebrows," the boy said.

He had blond hair and small blue eyes that didn't look very friendly. Even while he was talking, he was chewing on his fingernails.

"Peter," Dr. Ring said with his calm voice. "We only make encouraging comments."

"Well, it's hardly a bad thing," Peter muttered.

Erin had her hand on her face now and was forcing a smile. "I went shopping with my mom. Also got an A on a math test, which as you know is totally not my forte. That's really it."

"And did you work on our homework from last session?" Dr. Ring asked.

"Yes," she said. Her smile was gone in an instant. "I focused hard."

"Good," he said. "We'll get back to mindfulness later. Sara? Did you have a good week?"

He is always encouraging me to talk to more people, but a circle of staring crazies was not the time for a major lifestyle change. The whole group was looking at me. I shook my head.

"She doesn't talk," Erin offered.

"Are you shy?" Peter asked, but it sounded like he meant, "Are you stupid?"

I shook my head again.

"We only ask questions when they are invited," Dr. Ring said. "But to avoid confusion, Sara does not speak very much. She is here to learn, as we all are. Strength in numbers, right?"

They were still staring. Erin and the mean boy and the others. I didn't want to be stared at. I didn't want to talk or listen or even be around more crazies. Wasn't one of us enough? What if we made each other worse? What if I got mean like Peter or my eyelashes all fell out like Erin?

Hanging out with crazy kids seemed like a bad way to

become normal. I wondered if I should add a rule on the subject. Too late now.

I tried to stay calm, but it's hard once the bad thoughts start going. My body does strange things without me telling it to, and they don't just stop when I say stop. My skin gets hot and prickly. My throat dries up. My chest goes tight, like someone is sitting on it, or maybe filling it up with concrete. And I say, "Stop!" but it just keeps going, and I can never explain that to my parents. It happens every day. It gets tiring.

But I didn't want to show what I was to these strangers. Not if I could help it.

So I stood up and walked out.

I heard Dr. Ring calling after me and Peter asking, "What did I say?" but I ignored them and went into the waiting room. I sat down there because my mother wouldn't let me leave until the session was over. At least I would be alone. I put my head into my hands and tried to breathe for a minute even as my lungs tried to squeeze all the air out. What were normal kids doing right now? Playing video games? At a sports game? Maybe just hanging out with friends. Normal friends. I was pretty sure they weren't hanging out with crazy kids.

"You okay?" someone asked, dropping into the seat beside me.

It was Erin. I tried to act normal and nodded, but I knew I was breathing fast. I shoved my trembling hands under my legs. Dr. Ring was watching me from the doorway. I thought he might say something, but he just nodded at Erin and went back inside. He left the door open.

"It's tough to start," Erin said. "It's all, like, 'why are you crazy,' and Peter is *such* a boy, and well, you know. But it gets easier. I barely used to talk. Don't give me that look, I wasn't always this loquacious. Anyway, take the night off. Come and try again next week. It'll be better."

I shook my head.

"Think about it," she said, shrugging. "You want to hang out this weekend?"

I looked at her, confused. She picked up a magazine but kept talking instead of reading.

"Saturday night, maybe. I know it's hard to believe, but I don't have plans yet." She put the magazine down. "Do you have a cute older brother? If not, maybe we could wear pajamas."

I opened my mouth, and then just shook my head again.

"Perfect. Pajamas it is. What do you have anyway? Just the mutism? You on pills?"

I nodded.

"Same," she said. "An antidepressant. Do I seem bummed to you? Well, I'm not really depressed. It's for anxiety. This group is like a little anxiety party. Superfun. How many a day?"

I held up four fingers.

"Four different pills?" she said incredulously.

I nodded again and she whistled. "That's a lot. What for? All that for not talking?"

I shook my head, looked around, and then pointed at the bathroom.

She followed my gaze. "Something for the bathroom? A stool softener?"

I nodded. Then I realized that may have been too honest and my cheeks got hot.

She just laughed. "Hey, no judgment. No one likes a hard poop."

I smiled, which was strange because usually only Ms. Hugger and my dad could make me smile. I gestured to the open door to let her know she could go back into the session if she wanted.

Strangely, I wasn't sure that I wanted her to leave.

"Nah," she said, opening the magazine again. "I'll wait with you. Now, about Saturday. Your place, for sure. Mine is a total pigsty. Army brat, so we always have unopened boxes everywhere. Plus I have an evil brother. Say . . . seven? What's your number? Ugh, I am the worst. Just give me your phone. I won't text you too much. Just joking. I'll totally text you every day."

She punched the number in herself, and then leaned back and put her feet up on the coffee table. I did the same thing because it looked normal. We stared at the far wall, and she talked the whole time and didn't even notice when I chewed my nails or tried to breathe—and if she did, she didn't seem to care.

When I got home, I read my list of normal rules before bed, whispering like usual so my parents wouldn't hear. But it felt different today. I had plans for the weekend. Me. Sara.

My stomach did a little flop, but then I realized something. I jumped out of bed, turned the lights on, and grabbed my list. Flipping to the second page, I took out a pen and grinned.

~~19. Make a friend~~

CHAPTER 5

SEVERAL CONVERSATIONS
(SORT OF)

At school on Friday I told Ms. Hugger about Erin. She was excited. We even talked a little about what girls did when they hung out and she gave me some ideas. Crafts. Movies. Gossip.

"What should we gossip about?" I asked, writing down some notes.

Ms. Hugger laughed. "Anything. We used to gossip about boys, mostly."

"Boys," I said slowly, writing that down. "Like, the anatomy?"

She coughed. "What? No . . . not the anatomy. I thought we had moved on from that."

Oh yeah . . . remember when I mentioned the incident about the internet? That was one.

The school librarian, Mrs. Yeltson, caught me researching

the male anatomy once. I wanted to tell her I like to research everything equally, but she wasn't on my talking list. So she just said naked men had no place in the library and put me on probation, which meant I couldn't use the internet anymore without Ms. Hugger supervising. Mrs. Yeltson was not very friendly.

"I am sure Erin will take the lead," Ms. Hugger said, turning back to the whiteboard. "But I think this is great. A friend your age is just what you need. Now, we were on to history—"

"Ms. Hugger?"

She glanced back, the marker halfway to the board. "Yes?"

"What do I do if a Game starts?"

Ms. Hugger walked over and put her hand on my shoulder. "Then you just take the time you need. Erin will understand. You couldn't ask for a better friend than someone who gets you."

I was still nervous, but I just nodded. "Okay."

She squeezed my hand and started back for the board. I thought of something.

"If you ever want to gossip about Sven, I'm available. Just his personality. Not his—"

"Thank you," Ms. Hugger said, biting her lip. "I will keep that in mind."

I was lying in bed at two in the morning, still wide awake.

When I had gotten home from school, I already had six text messages from Erin.

Hey, bestie! How you doing? Can't wait to hang tomorrow!

Ugh, my teacher is SUCH a pill.

What you up to? Lunch here. Tuna? I swear my mom wants me to eat alone.

Do you ever think that boys were created just to annoy you?

Text me back, girl!

Home finally. Can't wait to hang! Be there at seven. What should I wear?

I just typed:

Learning, I don't get it, eating and I like tuna, no, here I am, clothes.

I assumed that covered everything, but she was silent for a bit and then texted:

You are SO weird. I love it. See you tomorrow, bestie.

Of course, that confirmed that Erin really was coming over tomorrow night. My mom was happy about it too, maybe even more than Ms. Hugger. I had been excited too, but now I wasn't so sure. I didn't really know how to gossip. What kind of crafts did she like to do? What kind of crafts did *I* like to do?

"You can't do normal things," my brain reminded me. "You can't go a day without a panic attack. You can't go an hour without a quiet break. You can't go a minute without being afraid."

My thoughts started to pick up speed. It was true. What was I thinking, agreeing to this?

I stared at the shifting shapes on my ceiling—the shadows of tree branches like fingers that reached for me when the wind blew. I looked around the bedroom. Calm down. Calm down.

My room was an underwater library. It was literally designed to calm me down. The walls were blue and the trim was printed with orcas jumping out of the water. There were framed pictures of dolphins and even a great white shark beside my desk. That probably wouldn't calm down most people, but from straight on they looked like they were smiling. One whole wall was bookshelves, with a few dusty stuffed animals beside it. There were 619 books in my room, spread across fourteen wooden shelves that my dad had built and carefully organized by category and then by last name. No dust.

Thinking about the books or the ocean sometimes helps. But it was too late today.

My thoughts were rolling together. *I want to be normal I can fix this I can get better I can make a friend I can be an astronaut I can make Daddy proud I cannot breathe my stomach hurts I can be normal my throat is dry I cannot breathe am I dying am I dying I will never ever be normal.* And the voice saying it got louder. Me, I guess. My brain.

I could feel the anxiety coming. I had taken my nighttime

pills, of course. But they didn't always work. If they did, I guess I would be cured. It's part of the reason I want to stop—they aren't a cure. Just a Band-Aid. But the main reason is that normal kids don't take them. So if I want to be normal, I couldn't take them either.

In fact, it's rule number one on my list: *Stop taking your pills.* I hadn't had the courage to try yet, but I would one day.

The pressure on the chest was building. Headache. Hot skin. Shallow breath.

I wanted to cry.

All I wanted was to be normal. Like the kids on TV, and at school, and in my books. That meant no pills. It meant no Games. It meant no mayonnaise, and no quiet breaks, and no cinnamon on my popcorn, and no this, and more that. All the things that everyone knew but me.

"It's just a False Alarm," I whispered to no one. "False Alarm. It's not real."

But my breathing still wasn't working right. I tried to not have to think about breathing. That was a bad plan. I thought about it even more, and when I tried to make myself breathe normally, it seemed to stop altogether. I tried to remember that Dr. Ring said, "Your breathing can't just stop, Sara. Humans can't do that to themselves." But that was easy for Dr. Ring to say. He wasn't crazy.

Now it felt like I was breathing through a straw. I was sweating and tingling.

"Uh-oh," I murmured.

My throat closed and went dry. My head spun and my brain cried out for help. It screamed, "Run!" and "Hide!" and "Freeze!" My stomach turned, and my heart pounded so loudly it was all I could hear, and I couldn't shout because I had no air. So I lay there and got ready to die. And I was sad, but I was scared, too. *Would dying be better than this feeling?* I wondered. When the attack finally passed, it faded into a shadow, and I felt weak.

When it was done, I lay there, tired and spaced out and knowing that yes, it was just a False Alarm, and I wasn't dead, and I shouldn't have panicked. But yes, it would happen again.

Dad came home later. The front door opened slowly, and I listened as a bottle opened and he guzzled it. Creaking footsteps came up the stairs. He peeked in, a silhouette in the hallway.

"Hi, Daddy," I said.

He came closer and knelt beside my bed. It was so dark I could only see his eyes.

"Hello, Princess." He ran a hand through my hair. "You should be asleep. It's late."

"So should you."

"Yeah, you're probably right."

There was something new in his voice.

"Are you okay?" I whispered.

"Fine."

"You're lying. If I could see you, I'd know. Your face, please."

"Sara . . ."

"Face. We're playing the Blind."

The Blind was a game. You closed your eyes and felt the other person's face to guess how they were feeling. I was a very good player. He sighed and leaned forward.

I used both hands, finding his face in the darkness. I ran my fingers over his cheeks and eyes and stubble like a sculptor, giggling when his fuzzy upper lip prickled my fingers. His eyes were the answer. They were swollen and puffy.

"You were crying," I said.

He was silent for a while. "Daddies never cry."

"What's wrong?

"Nothing, Princess. I just wanted to say good night."

I didn't believe him, but Daddy was stubborn.

"Good night," I said.

"I love you. You know that, right?"

"Yes," I said, smiling.

"And you are perfect. You know that too, right?"

Like I said, I am not good with lying.

I didn't reply, and he hugged me and walked out.

The next day I went to the park. It is just a block away, and my parents let me go alone to read on the grass. Erin was coming after dinner and it was making me nervous, so I was going to bank some quiet time.

Naturally, I was ambushed.

"Hello, Sara."

I looked up and found James staring at me with his hands jammed into his pockets. I had forgotten how strange his eyes were. Big and brown and sad. His head was fully shaved now. It looked like an egg.

I stared back at him for a moment. It was not a yes-or-no question. It was a say-something-back kind of question, and I don't really do those. But he just stood there. I nodded.

He smiled. "You're a real talker, huh?"

I shook my head. Now he was getting it.

He sat down next to me and I frowned.

"That's okay," he said. "I don't talk much myself lately."

I looked at him with an expression that said, *That is ironic, James,* and he snorted.

"Well, not compared to you, I guess. Unless . . . are you deaf? Or mute?"

He tapped his ears, and I shook my head.

"Just shy," he said, nodding. "Fair enough." His hands were moving in his lap like he was building a tiny snowball. "I can leave if you want. I'm sorry to bother you."

His eyes really were sad, and I didn't want to be mean, so I shook my head.

"Cool. I was walking, and, well, I don't know. Lonely, maybe. You live around here?"

Nod.

"Yeah, I'm a few blocks away. What grade? Oh, right. Umm . . . sixth . . . no . . . seventh?"

Nod.

"Eighth for me. I'm at St. Paul."

Catholic. Made sense if he lived that close. I was in public school and wouldn't see him.

"I play basketball. You play anything?"

I shook my head vehemently and he laughed.

"Fair enough. You been seeing Dr. Ring long?"

Reluctant nod.

He looked me over. "You seem normal to me."

Ha. Nice crazy-gauge, rookie. I gave him a patronizing smile.

"Yeah, looks don't mean much," he said, staring out at the park. "Do I?"

I raised my eyebrows because I wasn't exactly sure what he was asking.

"Do I look normal?" he asked softly.

I thought about that for a moment. The sad eyes. The tight smiles. I shook my head.

He laughed. "You don't do the whole little white lie thing, do you?"

Shake.

"Good. Everyone else does. Can I sit here for a bit? I won't say anything else."

I hesitated. He really did look glum, so I nodded, and he smiled. We sat there and said nothing and stared at the grass. Then he just stood up, smiled at me, and walked away.

"Bye, James," I whispered, but only when he was long gone.

"I have to say, I didn't expect the ocean theme."

Erin was lying on my bed, looking around the room. I wasn't really sure what to do, so I was just sitting at my desk, following her gaze. I had never had anyone in there before, other than my parents. She had been studying the room for at least five minutes, and I was nervous.

"I was thinking black. Maybe like a Metallica poster. You're so quiet and grim." She swung her legs over the side of the bed and stared at me. She was wearing pink and yellow pajamas, and her hair was in big pigtails. "Maybe I was wrong. Are you sure you don't talk?"

I shook my head, which didn't really answer the question. To be honest, I wasn't really sure. I had never had a friend.

She nodded as if I had said something. "Selective mutism. I read up on it yesterday. It's all right. We're besties now, but we are moving fast. You have to get comfortable and so forth. It's a process. Well, where to start. My last name is Stewart. Boring, right? We moved here a year ago and I think we're staying for a bit; my dad is in the army, remember? My brother sucks—"

"Sara?" my mom said, poking in. "I brought some cheese and crackers."

Erin rolled over and propped herself on her elbows. "Mrs. Malvern, you are the best. Does Sara talk to you? No . . . so rude. Don't tell me." She turned back to me. "Sorry, bestie. Total privacy violation. I read up on it. Should we watch something? Let's pig out and watch Netflix."

My mom looked at her, then at me, barely holding back a laugh.

"Sara is having a busy day," she said. "First that boy in the park, and now a girls' night."

I gave her my strictest *that was confidential* stare, but she was already leaving.

"Cancel the Netflix," Erin said, jumping up and closing the door behind her. "Tell me everything. Or, you know, nod while I interrogate you. Boy. How cute? Nod once for very, twice for crazy cute. No. Let's start with his name. I need to build a profile. Nod once for Aaron."

"His name is James," I murmured.

I don't know what it was. Maybe it was the fact there are a lot of boys' names and we could have sat there for three days. Maybe I decided crazies were exempt from my no-talking rule, or that friends were an exception, or that I might as well knock off another rule. Number ten: *Talk to somebody new.*

Actually, I think I knocked off, like, three. It was a good start, but my throat was dry again.

She didn't say anything for a moment. Then she walked over and gave me a hug.

"You trust me," she said, face buried in my shoulder. "Now, James."

As she pulled away, her sweater rode up, revealing her hip. It was deeply bruised, mottled brown and green and black at the heart. The sweater fell over it again, hiding the view.

I opened my mouth, but closed it again. What did she say? A privacy violation. Right.

She still did most of the talking, but I talked too. We sat there for hours. I never asked about the bruise. Since I had never had a friend, I played it safe. I had to go to the bathroom to breathe a couple of times, and twice I started coughing when I didn't really need to, but Erin didn't seem to care. She just flipped through her phone while I went to the bathroom and launched right back into conversation the very second I was back. I had vaguely hoped she went to James's school, so she could tell me more about him, but she was in a public school too—she just lived in a different district.

When her mom picked her up, she gave me another hug, and texted a minute later.

Good night, bestie. Talk to you Thursday! Just joking. I will obviously text you 100 times before then.

I stared at the text that night as I lay in bed. I read it a hundred times at least.

I had hung out with a friend. Me. Sara Malvern.

My eyes got a little watery, but tonight, they weren't sad tears.

NOTE

You might be wondering when I officially got my nickname. You know . . . Psycho Sara.

For a while, I tried to pretend it was a superhero name. Like, *Watch out, robbers, Psycho Sara is here and she is going to get angry and you won't like that!* Yes, I stole it from the Hulk.

Anyway, after the whole smashing-the-mirror day I got special attention at school and started taking a few classes in the Crazy Box. Most kids don't get their own Crazy Boxes, but they decided I was a unique case: Socially I didn't fit in the normal classes, but academically I was ahead of everybody and would disrupt a larger special education class. So I got listed as an "exception," which would have been cooler with an extra "al" at the end.

In fifth grade I had a special education teacher named Mrs. Gregoriwich. She was supermean, and yelled a lot, and didn't let me take Sara breaks. One day she decided that I was ready to go back to regular classes, as long as she was there to supervise me. My parents weren't sure, but she was very convincing.

My new teacher seemed nice. I had pretty much

stopped talking a year before because talking got me in trouble, but it wasn't a full-out life strategy yet. So I just sat there for a few weeks and tried to act normal. It was hard. I kept getting hot. Restless. My thoughts would start spinning. Sometimes I felt like I couldn't breathe right. Sometimes I felt like I was in danger without knowing why or from who.

But I tried and tried because I wanted to stay.

It was tiring, though. Exhausting. And when you get tired, you make mistakes.

It started with a panic attack. I had gotten them before, but I didn't know much about them. As it was starting, I whispered to Mrs. Gregoriwich to let me go to the bathroom, and she said no, and it felt like my whole body was on fire.

"Please," I whispered.

"We just went thirty minutes ago—"

"But—" I tried again, keeping my voice down.

People were staring. *Daniel* was staring. Did I mention him yet? Stand by.

"Just sit still and listen—"

And then I screamed. Like a shrill, bloodcurdling scream. Was it a good reaction? No. Did it scare my classmates and almost make Mrs. Gregoriwich fall over? Yes. Did I care at the time? No.

I screamed, and she hustled me out, and I went to the

bathroom to die but surprise! I lived, like I always do. And that was that. I got my new nickname, I went back to the Crazy Box, and I never joined regular classes again. One scream and you're a psycho. It's all right. It's just a temporary thing. As soon as I get better, I'm going back. Maybe I'll get a new nickname.

Smart Sara. Super Sara. Splendid Sara. Doesn't matter.

Sara—just *Sara*—would be fine.

In fact, it's all I want. Just plain, normal Sara.

Yeah. That would be more than fine.

CHAPTER 6

NOT ALL GAMES ARE FUN

We have school assemblies once in a while. An author visit, or a fire safety demonstration, or a talent show. On Monday morning we had an anti-bullying presentation, and Ms. Hugger decided we could attend.

I always had to sit on a bench with the teachers, even though the other kids were cross-legged on the floor. They organize the grades in seated lines from kindergarten at the front to eighth grade at the back. The whole school was there, so there wasn't much room. I was close to the eighth graders, and I was being careful not to make eye contact with anything but my shoes.

The presentation seemed nice. It was about helping each other and combatting bullying with teamwork. But two girls were not listening. They were looking at me and whispering.

Ms. Hugger was half watching and half texting, so she

didn't notice. I tried to do the same. But I could hear them and feel them looking. I started to feel fidgety and hot, and that always means my brain is about to pick a Game. She spins a big wheel and we both wait to see what it will be, except she always sees it first and gets to tell me. Today it was the Danger Game.

Now I could hear the girls very clearly.

"What a freak," one girl said.

She was nearly shouting, but no one else heard her.

"Completely crazy. She shouldn't be here."

"She could hurt someone," the other girl agreed.

They were smiling at me like two hyenas.

"We should do something about it," one girl said.

It's just a Game, I told myself. *It's not real.*

"I agree," said the other. Suddenly she had a knife or at least a flash of light on something metal, and then she was standing up. "There is no time like the present."

My brain won the Danger Game. I stood up and burst through the gym doors and heard laughing. I kept running all the way to the Crazy Box. Then I locked the door and breathed.

Ms. Hugger appeared at the glass. I let her in and she gave me a hug.

"Was I right this time?" I whispered.

"No, Sara," she said quietly. "You are never going to be right. It's not real."

"I saw a knife."

"You didn't."

"They wanted to kill me."

"They don't."

I breathed again and sat down at my desk. We were both quiet for a little while.

"Do you ever lie to me, Ms. Hugger?" I asked.

"No."

"Never?"

"I would not lie. But that doesn't mean I can answer every question."

I wanted to believe her, but it was time for a test.

"Have I gotten better this year? Have I made any progress?"

Her eyes moved. "We have accomplished a lot—"

"Not my academics. Me. My brain. Have I gotten any closer to going back to normal classes?"

"Sara . . ."

"Tell me."

"No," she said finally. "I'm still not sure you're ready for that."

I nodded and put my head down. Ms. Hugger was telling the truth, and I knew that was real and I could relax. The Game was over. I was very tired, and Ms. Hugger let me fall asleep.

* * *

As usual, on Tuesday night Dr. Ring knew all about my freak-out. I sat facing him on the corduroy couch and waited as he got his notes in order and turned to me, pen at the ready.

"So, Ms. Hugger tells me we had a round of your 'Danger Game.'"

I was really starting to regret telling them about the Games.

"Maybe," I admitted.

"Which, as we know, is a—"

"Schizophrenic episode." I was staring at my hands in my lap. "My name is better."

"You know I never approved of the names."

"You may have mentioned that once or twice."

"Why don't I approve of them, again?"

I sighed and recited his usual speech.

"Because they individualize my problems, as if I am the only person who has them, when, in fact, they are very common issues with scientific names and established treatments."

He put the pen down. "And you thought those girls wanted to hurt you?"

"I . . . thought I heard something."

"And the first step should be?"

I paused. "To assess likelihood. If that fails, talk to Ms. Hugger."

"And what did you do?"

I paused again. "Ran back to the Crazy Box."

Dr. Ring stood up. That was unusual. He walked over to the bookshelf and began to pace in front of it, his hands clasped neatly behind his back. He did that for nearly a minute in silence.

"Do you remember what you said to me the first time we met?" he asked finally.

That had been a few years ago, when my parents decided to try a new doctor.

"No."

"You said, 'Please make me better.' And I told you what I always do. That you are who you are. That you can't set unrealistic expectations. That I can't turn you into someone you are not. That instead we must work toward becoming the best version of ourselves."

I closed my eyes. I did remember that. It was when I started my rules. I decided that if no one else could help me, I would have to do it myself. That I would become Normal Sara.

"I remember," I said.

"You are fighting me at every step. If I tell you to walk, you run. Whisper, you shout. Sometimes it seems you are doing the exact opposite of what I prescribe. And I know why."

"Because you can't help me."

"No," he said. "It's because you blame yourself. Despite everything you know."

I felt a little stirring of anger. Sometimes it flares up, like someone blew on some coals. Not often. Dr. Ring said

I had volatile emotions. Part of the bipolar disorder.

But I didn't get angry much. It never ended well.

"Who do you want me to blame? God? I tried that, and He didn't do anything either."

"There is no one to blame. It could be genetics. Could be luck. It doesn't matter."

I stood up, hands balled at my sides, trembling all over. "Of course it matters!"

He turned to face me. "You need to stop trying to find someone to blame. You need to work on managing your issues—"

"I want to be better!" I screamed. I hadn't shouted in here in months. But all of my control was slipping away now. "I don't want this anymore! I don't want a brain that is trying to hurt me. I am always afraid of what my brain will say to me. Always. And nobody can help me!"

The last part spilled out with tears that I didn't even know were coming.

"Of course they can," Dr. Ring said calmly. "But it will be much easier for people to help if you let them."

And then I was crying. I wanted to believe it was that easy. But all these years, and I wasn't getting better. I was still in the Crazy Box. I was still Psycho Sara. He waited for me to cry myself out. Soon I was back on the couch, quiet again.

"So what do you want me to do, exactly?" I asked finally, eyes on the floor.

"I want you to start liking Sara Malvern."

I snorted. "Why would I possibly like myself? I'm a total nut."

"That's something I want to help you find out," he said. "Until you do that, it's not going to get better."

"I don't," I said finally. "I'm sorry. I don't like myself. Not like this. I won't. Ever."

He nodded. "Then we had better find a reason to start."

CHAPTER 7

A QUESTION I DON'T LIKE TO ANSWER

On Wednesday night, Erin came over again, and we sat in the living room and put on *The Notebook*. I had never seen it, and Erin pretended to faint when she found out—I think she was pretending—and said we had to watch it immediately because it was "stupidly cute and Ryan Gosling is my whole entire heart." Very little of that made sense to me, but I agreed to watch it.

My dad was out, my mom was in the kitchen, and Erin was mostly just talking.

"So," she said through a mouthful of popcorn, "are you picturing James right now?"

I spit my own popcorn out. "What?"

The two main characters were kissing. I flushed.

"Well, just swap out Ryan Gosling for James," Erin went on. "Keep the kissing, though. Oh, don't look so scandalized. Sometimes I forget you're a year younger."

"You said you just turned thirteen last month," I murmured.

"And you're still twelve. Things change. I mean, do you think I always wore this amazing pineapple lip gloss?" She took it out of her pocket. "Yeah, I know. I always did. Never mind James. Who needs boys? Other than Ryan Gosling. So, I looked into selective mutism again—"

"I don't have that," I interrupted. "Not officially. I . . . don't want another name."

It came out a bit sharper than I intended, but she just nodded, smiling.

"Right. I get that. Well, I just want you to know you can talk to me about anything. Like, code of silence, lockbox, never-speak-of-it-to-anyone kind of thing. And I hope I can do the same. Besties have to be able to trust each other. It's the foundation of best friendship. Complete trust."

I nodded. "Sure. Do you want to talk about your trichotillomania?"

I had done my own research on my mom's laptop. She let me use it supervised so I could go on the internet. It was a hair-pulling disorder. Anxiety-related, like panic attack syndrome or OCD or my diagnosis: general anxiety disorder. Her hands went right to her eyebrows. She was still smiling, but I could see her lips quiver for a moment as she slid her fingers down her face and then back to her side. I am not good with people, but I could see that I had hurt her feelings.

"Sorry," I said quickly.

"No," she said. "Don't be sorry. I can't go blathering away about other people's issues and just pretend like Erin Stewart is all hairy fairy." She frowned. "That did not sound right."

"Hunky-dory?" I offered.

"Right. Anyway, I guess my ultrasleek eyebrows gave it away? Or my luscious lashes?"

I opened my mouth, paused, and closed it again. "Umm—"

"I know," she said softly. "It's hideous. I am reminded by every stupid reflection."

"It's not hideous," I said. "Why do you do it?"

She hesitated. "I don't know. It just kind of . . . happens. Sometimes not for a few days. Even a whole week. And then all of a sudden I'm in the bathroom again. And I'm picking, and I'm crying and thinking don't, and I do it anyway." She glanced at me, then softly ran her finger over her right eyebrow. "I did it before I came. I'm so stupid . . . I don't even know why. I felt okay today. Can you tell?"

I looked at her eyebrow. There were so few hairs anyway— but the right one was nearly gone, and it was a bit red from where she had pulled. I thought about how much it might hurt.

"A little," I said.

"Yeah. I try. Trust me. I try to read or walk away and even

when I finally get in front of the mirror, I still fight it for as long as I can. But I just . . . need to do it. Or think I need to. It makes me feel better for a second. Dr. Ring says it's a strategy to deal with my anxiety. Like a control thing. It's funny, because it feels like I have no control over it at all. Tricked by my own brain."

"I know what that's like. Doing things that you don't want to," I offered.

"Yeah, but at least you're beautiful. Black hair, perfect skin. You're like a prom queen."

I gingerly felt my face. Only my parents had ever said I was pretty. "I don't think—"

"Oh, please. Do you really think James just wants to chat? You don't even talk to him." She whirled on me. "You don't talk to him, right?"

"No."

"Good. Boys can't be trusted. Anyway, yes. I pull out my lashes. And eyebrows. And sometimes hair. I hate it, and I try to stop, but haven't figured out how yet. I'm a classic nut."

Without thinking, I reached out and squeezed her arm. "Same."

Erin leaned into me. "That's why we make a good team. I did have some friends before. Tamara. Kaya. They got weird. Didn't like the hair-pulling." She sighed. "They stopped inviting me places. And then it all got worse. We moved again, and I didn't really try at my new school. I could see them

mostly to Sad Sara, and he seemed to skip to Angry
His eyes were small and hard.

r. Ring nodded. "I remember. But you're working hard
l with it."

Yeah. Two pills a day. I still punched a hole in the wall."

Do you want to talk about that or save it for an individ-
ssion?"

Peter folded his arms. "I'm a crazy idiot. That's what my
aid. What else is there?"

There were a few murmurs around the room. Erin pulled
n eyelash. She didn't have many to spare. I fought the urge
hew my own nails. *Crazy idiot.* Sort of like Psycho Sara. I
d almost hear them say it. Ashley and Taj and all the others.

"That's an interesting point," Dr. Ring said. "Sometimes
ple call us names. They call us crazy. Retards. Freaks. Even
chos. How does that make you feel?"

He looked at me when he said it, and I decided my shoes
re interesting today.

"Like a freak," Peter said. "What do you think?"

"Erin?"

I glanced at her. Her fingers strayed near her left eyebrow.
e put her hand down.

"Yeah. Like . . . that."

"Sara?" he said. "Is that how you feel? Like their names
e all true?"

I thought about that. I thought about Taj and Ashley and

looking at me like I was a freak. It's hard to get started, you
know?"

"I never had any friends."

She looked at me. "Ever?"

I shook my head. I could feel my cheeks getting warm.
Not a Game. Just embarrassment.

"Well, you got one now," she said. "And you're stuck with
her."

I shouldn't have said anything. It was always safer to keep
things to myself. But it had been bothering me, and we were
friends, after all.

"How did you get that bruise on your side?" I asked.

She pulled back. Her hands went to her sweater, pulling
sharply at the bottom, as if it was riding up now. She moved
over a bit, and now she looked wary.

"When did you see that?" she asked stiffly.

"Last time—"

"It's nothing," she cut in. "I fell. Just, well, it's weird. I
mean, it's under my shirt."

I was confused now. Alarmed. She looked so offended I
thought she might walk out.

"I didn't mean—"

"It's fine," she said, smiling. But it was a different smile.
"Stupid fall. It's better now."

She turned back to the movie. We finished it, but she
didn't talk much anymore. By the time it was over, she had

already texted her mom to come and get her. She said bye and left without a hug. I watched the red taillights vanish down the street and went back to the couch.

"And that is why you don't talk," I whispered to no one.

I texted her saying Hey! the next morning, but got nothing back. All day I wondered what I had done wrong. The good news was that it was a Thursday. I didn't have to wait long to find out.

When I got there, Erin was already in the office, sitting in the circle of chairs. She looked at me, and I paused at the door. I wondered if I should leave. I started to turn away, but then I felt a hand on my arm, pulling me out to the lobby. I turned and found Erin staring at me, eyes watery.

"I'm sorry—" I said.

She gave me a hug.

"I'm such a diva," she said. "I'm sorry. I get so moody. I blame the craziness. It was nothing. I was being a pill. My evil brother always says I am. Are we good? Please say yes."

I smiled. "Yes."

"Good," she said, exhaling. "I thought I was back to no friends. I hated that phase."

"Did you ever try anyone else in the group?"

I had been thinking about that last night. Had any of them said something wrong?

"Well, Peter is about as bad as my brother. Mel said she

---

lives too far away to hang out, even where I lived, which was telling. Ar too much."

I bit my lip.

"Don't even say it," she said, gr back into the office and slid her seat cl sitive about . . . body stuff," she said, lo effect of pulling my hair out and lookir have to put up with me anyway, bestie.

Mel, Peter, and Taisha were watchin

Dr. Ring cleared his throat. "Who wa

Peter was busy chewing a nail again. to know?" he muttered.

Erin leaned close to my ear. "Peter is

I had figured that out already.

"I think he may have an anger issue—

"I'm trying to talk here," Peter said lo

"Easy, Peter," Dr. Ring said in his m "So, how was your week?"

Peter turned his glare on Dr. Ring. "It other week."

"Why?" he asked, pen at the ready.

"Because I have bipolar disorder, remem

Oh, great. We were bipolar buddies. I he fidgeted while he spoke, his fingers always always itching to chew a nail. I could see som

---

I wen Peter.

D to de

"

ual s

dad

out

to

cou

pe

ps

we

S

a

their faces when they called me names. I nodded and had to fight back tears. I wasn't sad because of Taj and Ashley. I mean, it's not nice when people call you retard, but it is worse when you say it to yourself. And I did that a lot. In the Crazy Box. In front of the mirror. Retard. Freak. Psycho Sara.

I was the worst bully of them all.

"Words can hurt us," Dr. Ring said. "I am sure we have all felt like that before. But no one here is a freak. You are perfectly normal people dealing with some common challenges."

Normal. That word hung in the room. It was a lie. I was still far from normal.

For now.

"What do you know?" Peter said. "You're a Muggle."

I looked up. Maybe Peter wasn't a total loss.

"You know I don't like you referring to people as Muggles," Dr. Ring said.

"Non-crazies," Peter corrected, folding his arms. "You get to be normal. I'm sure you guys can deal with a nickname. It's better than the ones I get. Spaz. Peter Pills. Crazy Idiot."

"Peter Pills has a bit of a ring," Erin mused.

"No one here is crazy," Dr. Ring said, making some notes.

Erin frowned. "I thought that was the point?"

"We are getting off-topic," Dr. Ring said. "I thought we could focus on a theme today that was brought up earlier. Let's discuss these assigned labels and how we can diminish their effect on us. In fact, I would like you to think about how to label yourself in a helpful manner."

"Oh, super," Peter said.

Dr. Ring spent the rest of the session telling us we weren't freaks. I don't know if anyone believed him. I didn't. On the way out Erin fell in beside me, a little more somber than usual.

"Wasn't that fun?" she asked. "*We are all normal people.*"

The other kids were getting into waiting cars. My mom was sitting in the van reading.

"See you Saturday?" Erin asked. "Want to do something during the day, too?"

I hesitated. I hadn't actually put a plan together or anything, but somehow I had sort of decided to go back to the park to read. It was an off-chance meeting. Probably just a onetime thing. But I was hoping for another. She stopped, looking at me suspiciously.

"James?" she said.

"I didn't make any plans—"

She sighed deeply. "I will be at your house at seven. Bring me stories."

She turned and ran to meet her ride. I did the same, climbing into the van.

"How was it?" my mom asked, glancing up from her cell phone.

"Enlightening."

"What did you learn today?"

She always liked a summary.

I paused. "That I am a Mudblood."

"Excuse me?"

"Two Muggle parents, one crazy daughter. Like Hermione, but less magical."

As we drove away, my mom seemed to be trying to figure out a proper response.

"Dr. Ring said that?" she said at last.

"No," I said, giggling. "Another crazy boy. He calls normal people Muggles."

She made a face. "I don't want to be a Muggle."

"Well, if you want to be a witch—"

"Sara!" she said.

"I said witch!"

"Oh." She settled in again. "So, that's really all you learned?"

I drew a little smiley face in the condensation on the window.

"Well, I also learned that I should probably stop calling myself a retard."

Mom was silent for a long time. "Yes, I think that would be a good idea."

I finished the smiley face and drew long hair like mine.

But the reflection behind it wasn't smiling, so I wiped it away with my sleeve.

CHAPTER 8

TWO SIDES OF SARA

On Saturday I went to the park at exactly one p.m. It was the same time as the last run-in, and I wanted to increase my odds. I sat on the grass and started reading Ms. Huggers's choice for book of the week, which was *The Invisible Man*. I had a feeling I was going to like it. Being invisible would have solved so many of my life problems.

I was nearly a quarter done and just thinking I should probably head home when I saw white sneakers above the edge of my book. I glanced up and saw James standing there, smiling.

"Hey, Sara."

He looked different today. His eyes were red and shiny, like wet glass.

"Can I sit?" he asked.

I nodded slowly because it had been my plan, but I tried

to look like I had to think about it. I wasn't sure what was coming over me. I didn't seek out human interactions. I avoided them.

He sat down, shifted to get comfortable, and stared at the playground.

"I wondered if you'd be here," he said. "I was hoping you would."

I kept my eyes straight ahead, trying not to look excited. My breathing was shallow. My chest was tight. But it made sense, and it was normal, and the thrill of that almost made me scream. But I had to stay normal with James. I set my book aside, waiting for him to continue.

He fidgeted, clearly uncomfortable. "So, I wanted to ask you about something. See if maybe you knew anything about it?"

I nodded.

"I had a panic attack yesterday," he said slowly. "I'd had one before, and Dr. Ring told me what it was. This one was in school. I was in the bathroom for an hour. I thought I was going to throw up, but nothing came out. I ended up lying on the floor. It was gross. I thought maybe I would die."

I had been there a million times. I was surprised. I knew he was seeing Dr. Ring, obviously, but I had never figured out why. He seemed normal.

I just nodded slowly.

"It passed," he said. "And I called my mom and got to go home. I'm so messed up."

"Panic attacks are not very nice," I murmured without thinking.

He stiffened. "You spoke!"

I flushed and shook my head. What was happening to me? I was out of control.

"You did!" he insisted.

I shook my head.

"Obviously, you speak," he said. "Please say something else."

I hesitated. I had started with zero the day after the screaming-in-class incident, and then added my dad, my mom, Dr. Ring, Ms. Hugger, and most recently, Erin. It had taken a long time, but I guess I was trending upward. I decided I could add James to the list. Normal people did talk, after all.

"Okay."

He grinned. He had very white teeth. I decided not to look at him again.

"That's a start," he said. "So . . . the panic attacks. Do you get them a lot?"

I had gone this far, so I just kept talking.

"Yes. I used to get even more before the medication."

He nodded and stared at the grass. "I guess the pills aren't working for me yet. Maybe a little. I guess I don't feel as sad all the time. Just when it hits, and I remember, it all goes crazy."

It finally clicked. That was why he seemed so normal. He was new to this.

"Somebody died."

James hesitated. "Yeah."

I looked at the plaid shirt. Not a father. It was too small. "Your brother?"

He squeezed his eyes and they leaked. "Yes."

"Was he older?"

"He was in tenth grade." His voice barely worked now. "He was in an accident."

"I'm sorry."

He wiped his eyes, but now his nose was leaking too.

"It was in a car. An older friend was driving. They went off the road. My brother's name was Kaylen. He was . . . my best friend. When he died, I got sad, and I didn't stop being sad after."

He cleared his throat.

"Did you lose someone too?" he asked.

I shook my head. "No. I was always . . . seeing Dr. Ring."

I was going to say crazy. But James wasn't crazy. He was sad. He wasn't used to panic attacks and Games and all my little tics like Erin was. I didn't want to scare him away.

His wiped his face again. "Does it get easier? Being like this?"

"Not really. No. But it's not forever."

Was that a lie? I hoped not. I wanted to believe. I needed to believe it.

"I feel like my brain is broken."

"It's hurt. It will get better."

He stared at the playground and kept rolling his hands together. "I miss my brother."

"Of course. But you just have to keep walking."

He gave me a strange look and seemed to be thinking about that. I really needed to stop talking so much. Dad always said I was overly honest.

He was silent for a minute. "You were nicer when you didn't talk," he said finally.

"I've heard that before," I admitted, flushing.

James ran a sleeve under his nose. "Can we still just . . . sit? I won't talk."

"Yes."

We sat there for a while. I didn't read, and he didn't speak. But it felt good anyway.

"You have a nice voice," he said at last. "Even if it's a little harsh."

I didn't know what to say to that. I just pursed my lips and kept staring at the park.

"Do you have Instagram or Messenger or something?" James asked.

I stared at him, confused.

"Like, on your cell phone?" he said.

"No . . . I'm not allowed to have data. Only texting and calling."

"Oh." He paused. "Can I have your number? I won't text you much or anything. Just, you know, if we want to make plans to meet at the park or something."

"Sure," I said.

My whole body was tingling as we exchanged phones and put in our numbers. I put in Sara Malvern as the contact, and he saw that and smiled and put in James Bennett.

I had given out my phone number twice now. I was rapidly becoming a socialite.

"Sara?" he said after a while.

"Yes."

"You going to be here next Saturday?"

I tried to hide a smile. "Maybe."

James laughed and shifted closer, and I was puzzled because I didn't really mind.

When I got home, I wrote another rule on my list. It was a little more specific than most:

138. Hang out with James again and DO NOT mess it up.

Erin questioned me about James for a solid hour. Finally, when she was satisfied, we watched another Ryan Gosling movie and ate popcorn. My dad watched some of it with us. I had to leave a couple times, but Erin had already termed them "Sara breaks" and told me to take as many as I needed. When you are trying to breathe, it's nice to know you can take your time.

At one point she reached forward to grab the popcorn bowl, and I saw a bruise on the base of her neck. It was new, but this time, I didn't say a word.

She left, and an hour later I was standing in front of the mirror after my shower. I do that sometimes. I stare at my reflection for a while. I guess it started after the mirror day. I think I wanted to see if I *looked* normal. But mostly I see the names written in the steam. *Freak. Psycho.* And today, I saw *ugly*, too.

I didn't usually think about that, but today I did. I even knew why. I kept thinking about James. It made my skin prickle and not in a bad way. But it made me want to be normal and cool and beautiful.

I didn't know how to . . . like someone. And so my brain did what it always does.

It spun the wheel.

I was still wet and my hair was draped over my shoulders like an oil slick. My face was thin and white and freckled. My eyes were pale green like overcooked peas. My incisors were like fangs, and there was an ugly yellow stain where I had chipped one. Today there was also a pimple on my collarbone with an inflamed circle, and it hurt when I squeezed it. I tried to calm down. Not today. *Please.*

But my brain doesn't need a lot of runway. I was too late.

I ran my fingers down my face and pulled tears from my eyes and snot leaked, and I gripped the counter so hard that my body shook. I was so tired of being sick. I was so tired of being Psycho Sara, and still she was there clawing and screaming and telling me I was stuck.

The panic attack came fast. It hit like ice and fire and my knees gave way. I put my head in the toilet and wretched. I gripped the sides and poured spit and tears into the bowl. When I couldn't wretch anymore, I curled into a ball by the toilet and hugged myself. I shivered and wondered if I might die.

My dad found me later and covered me with a robe and brought me to bed.

He stroked my hair until the fear faded to sleepiness.

"My princess," he said. "I'm here. I'm not going anywhere."

"Why won't it just go away?" I whispered.

"I don't know. I wish I could make it for you. Did you take your medications today?"

"I take them every day. But I don't want to anymore."

He sighed. "Why?"

"They don't fix me. And even if they could, I don't want them to. I want to do it."

"The pills help you, Sara. Why would you want more pain?"

"I don't. I just want to be normal."

He laid his hand on my cheek and smiled. "Now why would you want something like that? I wouldn't change anything about you. I wish it wouldn't hurt so much. But here we are."

I wiped my eyes, but they filled up again, and I left my hands over them like a mask.

"I want to give up sometimes," I said softly.

He pushed my hand away and took my face in his.

"You made me a promise," he said.

"I know."

He ran his fingers through my hair. Calloused and gentle.

"Sometimes it would be nice to get away," he said. "I know the feeling."

"Can we go together?" I asked.

"Of course," he said. "Where should we go?"

"A boat, maybe. We could go anywhere, then."

He laughed. "You always did love the ocean. A boat it is. Feel better, Princess?"

"Yeah. I think so."

He leaned down and kissed me on the forehead. "I'll wait until you fall asleep."

I fell asleep to his fingers in my hair, and I promised myself that I would feel better tomorrow, and play no Games. I said it like a prayer most nights, and I believed it most times, until the morning came again and I was still Psycho Sara.

NOTE
(REGARDING MY ONLY
CURRENT PROMISE)

My dad says it is important to keep your promises, so I think it is best to not make them. But I did make two promises in my life and they were both to him. The first one was to be good at the mall that day. That didn't work out very well. This was the second. We were watching television.

"I heard the kids were saying things to you today," he said.

His eyes were still on the TV.

"Yeah."

"Mean things."

"Yes."

"They called you Psycho Sara."

"Yes."

"You aren't . . . that."

I said nothing because I didn't like to lie to my father and I was a psycho.

He put his arm around me. When he spoke again, his voice was low.

"Sometimes I get worried about you. I can't always be there, you know?"

"Why not?"

"I just can't. Sometimes we all have to walk in different directions, even for a bit."

"Well, I can just go with you."

He laughed. "Most times. Not always. But you still got to walk regardless. You know?"

"Not really."

He smiled and mussed up my hair. "That's okay. Just promise me that even when I'm not there, you'll keep walking. In general. Even when things stink like they did today. Promise me you will keep walking, Sara."

"I promise, Daddy."

He pulled me into a hug and his eyes were watering. I didn't really understand why.

But a promise is a promise, and I would *not* break another one.

CHAPTER 9

FAILED EXPERIMENTS

have to pee."

Ms. Hugger looked up from her cell phone and sighed. It was Monday afternoon. Sunday had come and gone, and of course nothing at all had changed. I didn't get better. I played Strong Girl for most of the day and I was extra tired now as a result. Maybe I was still playing, actually.

"We worked on this," Ms. Hugger said. "You say, 'May I go to the bathroom?'"

"To pee."

"It's polite, Sara."

"May I go to the bathroom, madam?"

I was feeling sassy today, apparently.

She sighed again. "Let's go."

I am not allowed to go to the bathroom by myself, though Ms. Hugger at least waits by the entrance like a polite jailer.

The hallways were empty. I looked in through the little windows in the doors. They were like televisions showing classes sitting and learning and talking together.

"We really can try to join a class again one day," Ms. Hugger said.

"No," I replied softly. "I think that ship has sailed."

We passed the seventh-grade class, and I looked in and saw the lost boy. My favorite person to watch. Daniel Leigh. He had been in the class the day I screamed. I liked to watch him sometimes during recess. He always seemed like he was daydreaming. Counting nothing.

A part of me had always wondered if he was like me, but a lot better at hiding.

"Ms. Hugger?" I asked, pausing before I went into the bathroom.

"Yes?"

"Do you think I will ever have a boyfriend?"

She choked on air and looked at me. "What?"

"Do you think I'll ever have a boyfriend?"

She scratched her arm. "I . . . I don't know, Sara. I'm sure if when you're older . . ."

"Never mind the age. Me. Can I have a boyfriend?"

She hesitated. "I'm sure you will, Sara. If you want."

I didn't believe her.

I went into the bathroom and stared in the mirror. My mom had put my hair in a ponytail with a green scrunchie today. It made my face looked extra thin. But even if I was pretty, it wouldn't matter because the crazy would still be there.

I went to pee and sat in the stall so long that Ms. Hugger came to get me.

"I thought we would talk about self-identity this week," Dr. Ring said on Thursday evening. "A tricky subject."

Mel wasn't there this week, so it was just me, Erin, Taisha, and Peter. I had been the last to arrive and found myself directly across from Peter. He just gave me a sour look and chewed.

"What we think of ourselves is the lens through which we see the world," he continued.

"Mine is broken," Peter muttered.

"But you can fix it," Dr. Ring said. "*You* control self-identity."

I glanced at the rest of the group. Erin was picking eyelashes beside me. Her hair was pulled back into a ponytail with a black ribbon, and she was wearing a lot of makeup. It was caked on over her cheeks and chin like someone had built her from clay, and she had drawn on thin black lines in place of eyebrows and lashes. She was staring at the floor, looking distant.

"Erin?" Dr. Ring said, obviously noticing her distraction.

Erin paused with a stray eyelash between her nails. "Yes?"

"What do you think self-identity means?"

She spared the eyelash and seemed to consider that. "What I think about myself?"

"Partly. Also, *who* you are. You get to decide that. No one else. So, who are you?"

Erin fidgeted. I watched her and thought about the hair-pulling.

"Well, my name is Erin," she said slowly. "I'm in seventh grade and I like—"

"Deeper," Dr. Ring said. "Who are you at the core?"

It was quiet now. Even Peter was watching. Maybe he was asking himself like I was.

"At the core?" she said softly. "Rotten like an old apple."

I was stunned. Erin always seemed so happy and confident. But now I wasn't so sure. Maybe some people didn't talk to cover up their issues, like me. Maybe some talked more.

Without thinking, I put my hand over one of hers and squeezed. It was clammy and squeezed back. Peter seemed to notice. I saw his hand move. Just a twitch.

"That would make it hard to fit into the world," Dr. Ring said, giving me the slightest approving nod and making a note. "To think that everyone sees something that is sick or rotten."

"They do," Erin said. Her eyes were watering. "It's written on my face."

"Only through your lens," Dr. Ring said. "The rest of us

We walked outside, and she stopped, glancing at a red car by the curb.

"Got to go," she said quickly. "My dad hates waiting."

Before I could even say anything, she had darted over to the car. I caught a flash of a man in the driver's seat, staring straight ahead, and Erin for once saying nothing as they drove away. It all seemed a little strange, but I did lots of strange things. I just hurried over to the van.

"Well?" my mom said.

I considered that, thinking of another summary. One thing stood out . . . and oddly, it made me feel a little better.

"I'm not the only one who thinks she is a bad apple."

see a girl who is working through issues." He tu

"Sara, who are you at the core? Do you think you a

Or rotten?"

I wanted to shake my head. But that was a lie. I d

I was rotten. I *was* sick. That's why I was here. That's wh

to take the pills and make my list and try so hard. I noc

"Self-identity is created by us," he said. "A mental c

der is a disease like any other illness. The difference is

a person with a physical illness doesn't usually blame the

selves. They think they are unlucky to be sick. Not *responsibi*

They are right, of course. They're not responsible. And neithe

are any of you."

I looked at the floor and thought about that. He knew

what I thought. It had grown over time, somewhere deep

down the belief that this was my fault. That Sara Malvern

had *chosen* to be sick. And that made it all so much worse. It

made me guilty.

When the session ended, Erin and I walked out together.

"Do you think I'm rotten?" Erin asked softly.

"No," I said. "But I . . . think the same things about

myself sometimes. A lot."

She sighed. "I'm coming over tomorrow night. I want to

show you something stupid."

I looked at her, frowning. "Okay."

"You're going to laugh. It's just something I did . . . ugh.

Whatever. You'll see."

CHAPTER 10

STAR CHILD

We sat down for dinner on Friday night before Erin arrived. There was a vase of red roses on the table. We were having salmon, which was my father's favorite. Mom poured herself some white wine, which I guess meant the carpet was going to get a night off. I was getting excited.

She didn't pour Daddy any wine, but he had brought an open beer to the table. I could smell the beer on his breath and his eyes looked heavy. He sat and stared at the roses.

"Sara," my mom said. "How was your day?"

Another email. Ms. Hugger really was quick. I had fallen asleep at my desk after lunch and that was supposed to be math time. Unplanned naps always resulted in a discussion.

"Ms. Hugger emailed you," I said.

"She did. Are you getting enough sleep—"

"Where did you get the flowers?" my dad asked suddenly.

He still hadn't touched his salmon.

My mom looked at him. "At the grocery store."

"*Roses*," he said.

I looked at the flowers and back at him. He was tapping the table and staring.

"Yes," she said.

"Why roses?" he asked softly. "Strange thing to buy for a family dinner."

"They were on sale," she replied, giving me a smile and taking a bite. "Try the—"

"How much were they?"

She swallowed her fish and turned to him. "I don't recall."

"Get the receipt."

"I didn't get one—"

He stood up and swept the vase off the table. It shattered on the floor and roses and water went everywhere and I screamed. Mom ripped her napkin out of her collar and stood up, flushed.

"Why did you do that—"

"Don't bring roses to my table!" he screamed.

He finished his beer, stormed out of the house, and slammed the door behind him. My mother stood there for a moment, eyes watery, and then she started to pick up the roses and glass.

I took a bite of my salmon and tried to remember if we used to have nice family dinners.

"The salmon is good," I said quietly.

My mom looked back at me, walked over, and hugged me until the fish was cold.

When Erin got there, she marched straight to my room, gesturing for me to follow. She had a backpack on, and she seemed uneasy. Nervous, even.

When I had closed the door, she sat down on the carpet and opened her bag.

"Promise me you won't laugh."

"I promise."

She took out a folder with a bunch of papers and opened it up. Frowning, I sat down beside her, cross-legged, spotting scribbled notes and drawings. Most were of little stars.

"I read about it online first," she said, handing me a piece of paper. It looked like it had been printed off a website. The title said: *The Star Children Among Us.* "Then I did some research on my own. I read everything. Most of it is silly . . . but, well, there is some evidence."

"Star Children?" I asked, skimming down the page.

She flushed. "Basically, special kids that have alien DNA. They're supposed to be really smart and wise and different, obviously. I mean, it's all crazy, I know. People believe in this stuff, though. I don't. Well, I don't really. But I sort of liked the sound of it. You know. Special kids."

I didn't say anything. I read through some more printouts,

and her notes, and even something called the *3 Tenets of Star Children* that she had written. I read through them slowly.

1. You are a Star Child for life.

2. Star Children must always help each other.

3. Never be unkind to normal humans (unless they deserve it).

Erin was watching me and fiddling with her hands and straightening out the pile.

"I know," she said finally. "It's really dumb. But we were talking about what we thought of ourselves, and sometimes I like to think this is me instead. I just couldn't really bring it up at group with Peter staring at me like a gremlin. Now you probably think I'm an idiot. I really am."

I stared down at the tenets, thinking. I wanted to believe it too. I really, really did.

I used to lie in bed and wonder what I was. Not who. *What*. Because I could see other humans on TV and at school and at the park and they didn't seem like me. They didn't hear voices or get sad for no reason or feel like they couldn't breathe sometimes. So, I came up with other stories to make myself feel better. Sara was a superhero and she could sense danger. Sara was a friendly monster. God didn't like Sara. Sara was possessed. The stories were all the same.

Sara was special—that sounded better than crazy.

But I stopped that two years ago. I stopped imagining ways that I was special, because all I wanted was to be normal. I had to be normal. I didn't need tenets. I needed my normal rules.

But I also didn't want to offend Erin. I could see her watching nervously, ready to pluck.

"Okay," Erin said quickly. "Too weird. I know. Let's just never speak of it again—"

"I love it," I said, looking up at her and smiling. "I want to be a Star Child too."

It wasn't a lie. Not really. It was just pretending, so what did it matter?

She looked at me for a moment, maybe to make sure I wasn't making fun of her. Then she laughed and reached over and hugged me, squeezing so tightly that I started laughing too.

"You already are!" Erin said. "And that means we *always* have to help each other."

We spent the rest of the night going through the stories about other Star Children and making up our own. By the end of it, I decided to just keep pretending. It wasn't quite normal, but it was like a club. Even if it only had two members, it felt good. Well, some people claimed Mozart and Newton and a few others were Star Children too, but it seemed like they were all dead. Those were pretty awesome members, though. I even copied down her tenets so I would have them handy, and put them in my desk with the rules. I didn't share those. Somehow, I didn't think a Star Child cared about being more normal.

Eventually, we were both lying on the carpet staring up at the ceiling, shoulder to shoulder, the papers scattered around us like confetti. Her collection, and some new ones, too: my drawings of stars, and spaceships, and our theories that Star Children could still hang out with regular people, as long as they kept the secret of their true identity. I had added that one myself.

"What do normal girls do when they hang out?" I asked, imagining shapes in the ceiling stucco.

"Pretty much the same stuff. Well, we talked about slightly less weird things. Sometimes more weird. A few times we put on my mom's makeup and got yelled at."

"Oh. Do you miss doing that?"

"I don't know. I guess. That was before the hair-pulling, though."

She sounded sad, and that answered it for her. She missed being normal too.

I guess even a Star Child could feel lonely.

"Maybe I can help you get better," I offered. "Since we're Star Children and all."

She was silent for a long time, and then looked at me. "I would like that."

"I'll think of something. I'm good with problems, except for mine. I can help."

"Promise?" Erin asked, smiling.

I hesitated. I wasn't supposed to do this again. But maybe I could compromise.

"I promise to try."

CHAPTER 11

RULES AND REGULATIONS

After Erin went home, I said good night to my mom and went to bed. Daddy hadn't come home yet. I was worried about him. He was mad a lot.

An hour later, I was lying in bed, thinking instead of sleeping like usual. My pills were starting to tell my brain that sleep was nice and I could think more tomorrow. The pills always say encouraging things like that.

I just wish my silly brain would do it herself.

The front door opened and I heard soft footsteps. I slipped out from under the covers and crept downstairs, pausing in the shadows as the kitchen light flicked on. Daddy cracked a beer and went to the couch. I just watched him, silhouetted against the flashing light of the TV, not ready to say anything just yet. He drank more lately, and slept less. He was never a good sleeper, but now the dark rings around his eyes could have been tattoos.

I walked in and sat down beside him. "Hi, Daddy."

The blue light made his wrinkles deeper. I tried to remember it was Daddy, just tired.

"Hello, Princess."

He put his arm over my shoulders and pulled me in. He smelled like beer and body odor and cigarettes. I felt his chest rise and fall beneath my head.

"I'm sorry I ruined dinner," he said in a low voice.

"It's okay," I said. "I was never a rose person myself."

He snorted. "How was your night with your friend?"

"It was fun."

"Good," he said. His voice was quiet. Hoarse. "I'll be here next time."

"Okay."

His head was rolling a little and I waited as he leaned into me more and more.

"What did your mother say about the roses?" he murmured.

I realized he wasn't talking to me anymore. Not really. He was half-asleep.

"Nothing," I said. "We had a nice dinner."

"That's good," he said.

Then his eyes were closed and I quickly let myself out from beneath him. He muttered something and lay there like he was dead. I took the beer out of his hands and laid a blanket over him. Then I just watched him for a while and listened to him snore.

I remembered that he used to tuck me in every night and read me stories. Tonight I sat beside him in the blue and dark, and instead of a story I got snoring. It was better than nothing. My dad and mom weren't happy anymore. That was obvious. Maybe it was about me.

One more reason to get better, as if I didn't have enough.

On Saturday, I headed for the park promptly at 12:45 p.m. This time, I didn't make it.

"Hey, Sara."

I looked back and saw James jogging to catch up. He had his hands jammed in his jean pockets, and a plaid shirt collar was poking out beneath a bomber jacket. He soon fell into step.

"Hey," I said.

My cheeks were warm and probably flushing, but I blamed it on the cold.

"You up for a walk instead?"

"Sure."

We walked by three houses in silence. The leaves were all red and orange now, both the ones on the branches and the growing skirts around them. Our steps made soft crunching sounds.

I wasn't sure if I was supposed to say something. Was he

waiting for me? I tried to think of something clever to say, but nothing came to mind, so I just walked and waited and smiled.

"How was your morning?" he asked finally.

"Just read, mostly. Pretty quiet."

"Yeah," he said. "Well, no, actually, not for me."

He still had his hands in his pockets and he was walking slowly, so I walked slower too.

"Some days are better than others. But today I went into his bedroom. Dr. Ring said it would be good for me. To face my fears or whatever. So I thought I would give it a try today."

"He says a lot of stuff like that," I said. "That we must face what we fear."

"I don't know . . . I just started to cry. Didn't work."

He was staring straight ahead, and it sounded like tears were welling up. His voice was catching. I knew the sound and the feeling. A little ball in the throat that kept sneaking upward.

"I think it's supposed to work slowly," I said in my best comforting voice.

He glanced at me. "Did it work for you? Facing your fears?"

I answered without thinking. "No. Not really."

"Why?"

I paused. "Because I am afraid of myself."

We walked for a little while. He seemed to be thinking

about that. I wanted to take it back. I was supposed to be acting normal. It wasn't normal to be afraid of yourself. Stupid
Sara.

"Yeah," he said. "I don't know how it works, then."

The wind picked up and I zipped my coat to my chin,
pinching the skin.

"Your last name is Malvern, right?"

"Yeah," I said, frowning. "How did you know that?"

He paused. "I asked a friend of mine about you. He goes
to your school."

I felt my stomach drop. Skin prickle. All of that for nothing. All my trying.

"Who?"

"He's in eighth grade. Doesn't matter. I just asked if he
knew a girl named Sara. I didn't say how I knew you or anything. Just what you looked like." He glanced at me. "He, uh,
knew you."

"By a different name?" I asked quietly.

"It's stupid—" James started.

"What name did he use?"

"Well, he knew your last name. Malvern. But he said they
call you . . . Psycho Sara."

I kept my eyes on the sidewalk. Trying not to cry.

"Yeah," I murmured. "They do."

"He said you didn't talk. Learned in your own class.
Didn't know much else."

We were still walking, even slower now, and I was thinking that last Saturday seemed like a long time ago. We stopped at a red light and waited even though there weren't any cars.

I thought maybe I would just go home. He probably wanted me to.

"What did you say?" I asked, not able to help myself.

"Nothing. I said it was stupid."

I took a deep breath. "You don't have to hang around—"

"I like talking with you," James said, grinning. "You get all this stuff."

"Firsthand experience."

He peered at me, as if trying to find something written there. "You seem normal."

"Lots of people do on the outside."

He laughed and squeezed my hand. "I guess we know better."

"Yeah," I said, pulling my hand away without thinking. "Maybe."

I immediately regretted pulling my hand away. I just . . . wasn't used to that. Erin was always hugging me now, but I didn't know James. Now I had ruined it. Of course I had. I ruined lots of things.

I felt my throat going dry. Not now. Please. Please not now. Pressure on my chest.

He put his hand in his pocket and he looked embarrassed. "Sorry, I shouldn't just grab—"

"It's okay," I said. "Sorry."

My face felt really hot now and I tried to smile. Tried not to grab my chest.

Tried not to fall apart right here in the street.

I caught a flicker of motion behind him and saw a group of kids walking toward us. James noticed them, and his expression changed. He straightened his back and moved away in one motion. There was now an extra foot between us, just enough that I couldn't touch him.

"I got to go," he said. "I forgot I told my mom I'd help her with something."

"Okay."

I tried to make my voice behave.

"See you next weekend."

He walked toward the kids, and I walked home by myself. There was a ball in my throat now, but I told it to go away. I wasn't going to cry. When I got home, I went to my room and opened my book and stared at it without reading.

He knew my nickname. And he was embarrassed of being seen with me.

I wondered if James would want to go on any more walks, or come to the park anymore. Erin always made me feel like crazy was okay. But James reminded me that I wanted to get better. He had some issues too, but he had normal friends and a normal life, and he would be normal soon. I wanted to be there with him.

CHAPTER 12.

FORGIVENESS IS EASY
IF YOU FORGET

School went by slowly that week. I was busy moping about a stupid boy whose name rhymed with "games," and I think I annoyed Ms. Hugger a few times. Or more specifically, every time I said anything.

My review of *The Invisible Man* was that he was "lucky." She wondered if I meant the part where he tried to launch a reign of terror, or attempted a murder, or if it was when he was beaten to death by a mob. Ms. Hugger can be sassy too, sometimes.

Home was quiet. Mom said work was busy, so she was coming home later at night. We were eating a lot of pizza. Well, one night we had fast food. Dad was taking more naps than ever, and there were so many beer bottles in the living room I had to be careful not to kick them on my way to the couch. Erin texted me every day, but I replied slowly and with short answers.

Despite all my efforts, despite trying to look and talk and act as normal as I could, he still found out who I was. I tried to calm down. It was okay. I just had to try harder. Much harder.

I went to my desk and threw the three tenets of Star Children aside to grab my rules. Then I started writing. *Hold hands with James. Smile more. Act cool.* I added more and more until my hand hurt.

Then I looked at all my rules for being normal, put my head on the desk, and cried.

It was a lot to remember, and I still had so far to go.

On Thursday night I came into group therapy last because my mom was home late from work and my dad had drunk so many beers I decided not to wake him up. I sat down next to Erin.

"Hey, bestie," Erin whispered. "You were extra quiet with the texting this week."

"Sorry," I said. "I was feeling . . . extra quiet."

She stared at me. "Did James do something?"

I didn't want to talk about it. "No."

She clearly didn't believe me. "Boys," she said, shaking her head. "Typical."

I smiled despite myself as Dr. Ring started the session. The theme was honesty.

"Everyone lies to themselves sometimes," he said. "We pretend we are okay even if we are not. We justify an action that we know is wrong. But if you are struggling with mental issues, lying can be dangerous. If you tell yourself you are fine, that means you don't ask for *help*."

"I don't want to be pitied," Peter grumbled.

"Everyone needs help sometimes," Dr. Ring said. "Even Muggles."

I laughed without thinking and clamped a hand over my mouth.

Dr. Ring grinned. "Well, I made Sara laugh. That is a first."

"Does that mean she talks?" Peter asked, frowning.

"None of your business," Erin jumped in. "I speak on her behalf."

"Easy, everyone," Dr. Ring said. "Erin, what does honesty mean to you?"

Erin seemed to mull it over. "Telling the truth, I guess. But, I don't really know who gets to decide what is true. I mean, I think *I* do. So I guess it's just acting like who I really am."

She glanced at me, and I wondered if she was thinking Star Children.

"Interesting . . . and I agree. Because of that, I think it means showing vulnerability, too," Dr. Ring said. "Nobody wants to feel vulnerable. But acknowledging our own weaknesses and allowing others to see them lets us get the help we need."

He turned to me.

"Sometimes we want to keep control, even when we can't. And that causes problems."

I looked at the floor. He and I had talked about that before. About my need to control my sickness and fix everything. Not talking to people unless I decided it was safe. Trying to stick to my rules. Pretending that everything that happened to me was *my* choice and *my* fault. He wanted me to be vulnerable. But I couldn't do that. Even the thought scared me.

If I gave up that little bit of control I held on to—that belief that it was my fault and I could fix it by myself without the pills—what would be left behind? I was barely holding on as it was.

When the session was over, Erin and I started for the parking lot together.

"So, do I need to beat James up?" she asked, cracking her knuckles. "Ow."

I smiled. "No. I'll let you know."

She pretended to karate chop the air. "Do it. I am a green belt. I think. I was seven."

"Are we going to hang out this weekend?" I asked hopefully.

"Obvi. Tomorrow or Saturday? Or both? Actually, I think it's my brother's birthday." She frowned. "Yeah. We're having a family thing Saturday. Boring. He really is the worst."

She paused, glancing at me as we walked outside.

"Did you . . . want to come?" she asked.

I felt a little flutter in my stomach. A new house. New people. It was an easy no.

But, she was my friend. Friends hung out at each other's houses even when strangers were there.

"Okay," I said. "But I probably won't talk much. You know, this time."

"I told my parents you were shy." She smiled, but she seemed uneasy. "It's at six, I think. I'll text you. It's going to be boring, but we can just go up to my room once the cake is all done."

"Okay."

She hugged me and headed for her ride. "See you Saturday!"

As I hurried to my mom's van, I smiled. I was going to a birthday party. At someone's house. That was number forty-one on my list: *Get invited to a party.* I'd added that one when I found an invitation to Ashley's party on the floor in the school hallway and realized I would probably never be invited to one unless I made some changes.

Maybe I could even stop by the park first in the afternoon.

And an optimistic little voice said, "Maybe you can be a normal girl and a Star Child."

It wasn't likely, but I clung to it anyway. Dr. Ring wanted honesty. I wanted hope.

I was losing that hope on Saturday afternoon. I had been sitting in the park for an hour, and it was cold enough that I was reading with gloves on, which is not easy. I had scared James away.

It shouldn't have mattered. I was used to being alone. I closed my book, cold nipping through the gloves.

And then James dropped onto the grass beside me.

"Hey," he said.

"Hi," I managed, fumbling the book.

"I should explain the other day—" James started.

I was supposed to play it cool, but Angry Sara decided to take the lead.

"You left pretty suddenly."

Why did my voice sound like that? It was like a whip. I had never even heard it before.

He fidgeted and scratched his neck. "I had to get home."

"You didn't want those people to see us together," I said.

Well, I was all in now. Angry Sara wanted to interrogate. I could see he wanted to lie more.

"It would have been hard to explain. No one knows I go to therapy but my mom."

"And they would have known I was crazy just by looking at me?"

"Well . . . no," he said. He must have been very itchy because now he was scratching his arm. "I just . . . well . . . Dion knew you right away. It just seemed easier not to go introducing people and all that." He sighed. "No, you know what? I shouldn't have done that. I'm sorry."

I raised my eyebrows.

"Dr. Ring said to channel my grief," he said, playing with his hands. "To make my brother proud. And maybe he meant into school and stuff, but I think also into just being a better person. And I like that idea."

"He is an optimist, that Dr. Ring."

I wanted to be mad or hurt or at the very least cold, but my resolve was breaking. He was so disarmingly . . . earnest.

"I won't do that ever again, okay," he said, and he stuck out his hand for a shake like we were signing an international treaty. "I promise."

I don't take promises lightly, but it wasn't mine, so I shook his hand and nodded.

"Fair enough."

He smiled, and I forgot all about it. I also noticed he was wearing a hoodie.

"Progress," I said, gesturing to his collar.

"And cold," he replied, showing me the plaid shirt beneath it.

It *was* cold. I zipped my coat up and shivered at the breeze that crept down my neck. We sat there quietly for a moment and let the wind do the talking for us. Normal for me, but he seemed especially somber. His eyes were locked on nothing, and the smile was long gone now.

"Everything all right?" I asked.

He forced a smile. "My mom. She started crying when she saw my shirt. She does that a lot. She asked me to stop wearing them because they remind her. And I said I wear them *to* remind me. I accused her of wanting to forget, and she cried more. And then so did I and left."

His voice was halting and hoarse. "I feel like such a jerk, you know. I know what she meant. I'm just . . . I don't know."

"What?"

"I'm acting stupid," he said, shrugging. "Even I know it."

"You lost someone. I think it's okay to act a little crazy."

He was silent for a long time. "I talk to him a lot. I just . . . start talking."

I saw tears coming down his cheeks. I didn't know how to console people, so I just waited.

He roughly wiped his face. "At night, mostly. I stand outside a lot. When the sky is clear. It's dumb, but I read one time that people used to think stars were people who died. I liked that."

I followed his gaze up to the blue sky. No stars but one.

"Well, we are made of stars," I said.

"What?"

"Star stuff. They create organic compounds like carbon in their cores. They shoot them when they go supernova and the compounds come to planets and they form lots of things, including us."

"How do you know that?" he asked.

"I like space. I read *Cosmos* last year."

He frowned and followed my gaze. "Sometimes I do feel small looking up there."

"It should make you feel big. Like a time traveler. The starlight you see isn't from now. It could be from a million years ago. Maybe more. There might have been an alien then, staring up, and if we had the right telescope, we might see it. It would be like seeing a ghost. But just for us. That alien was alive when it was looking up at us. So we are both alive, sort of."

He seemed to take that in for a moment. "So . . . they might see my brother one day, just walking around and playing ball with me in the driveway."

"They might."

James smiled. Then he turned to me. "When are you going to act crazy?"

"It'll be a surprise," I said, and that made me sad because it was true.

"Well, feel free at any time. I'm beginning to think it's just me."

We sat there for another minute or two, listening to the breeze.

"I should probably get going," I said. "My dad said be back in an hour. Two hours ago."

"Yeah," he agreed, though he sounded reluctant. "I guess I better go talk to my mom."

"What will you say?" I asked.

"I love you, I guess. And maybe that my brother is a star and that is just science."

I smiled. "That would be a good start."

When I got home, I went to my room and took out my rules. The tenets of being a Star Child were lying above them, but I skipped those, opened my old notepad, and started to read.

This time I stopped on one of them, and read it aloud again and again.

"Hang out with James again and DO NOT mess it up. Hang out with James again and DO NOT mess it up."

Then I crossed it off and smiled. Maybe I was getting better after all.

I was still staring at the rule when my mom poked her head in the door.

"Sara, we should go soon. You don't want to be late for the birthday party!"

My stomach knotted itself up into a pretzel. Well, I said I was getting better.

Now it was time to put that to the test.

CHAPTER 13.

HAPPY BIRTHDAY

Erin lived in a squat little house about fifteen minutes from mine. She said her family moved a lot into rentals, and that she never got too attached to anywhere. The house seemed perfect for that role: white siding, brown door, square lawn. It looked like a million other houses in the neighborhood.

My mom was supposed to drive me, but when my dad found out I was going to a birthday party, he insisted that he go instead. He didn't seem to approve. And now that we were in the driveway, he looked nervous. He kept looking at the house and me and the house again.

"You sure you want to go?" he asked.

He had both hands on the wheel, as if he was ready to drive away.

"No," I admitted.

My stomach was still clenched up, like someone had put it in a vise. I was making so much progress. Even a few weeks ago I couldn't have imagined going to someone's house for a birthday party. But now I realized just how quick it had been.

What if a Game started out of nowhere? False Alarm. Strong Girl. The Danger Game would be the worst of all in a house full of strangers. I had one of my nails between my teeth before I realized it, and my dad reached out and drew my hand away, squeezing it gently. He hated when I chewed them and always grimaced when he saw the nubs. He held my hand in his.

"You want to go get ice cream instead?" he said, smiling. "Just send Erin a text."

I hesitated. I wanted to go with him instead. It was safer.

But I thought back to sitting with James today. To that moment of reading my rules and feeling normal, and all of that was because I was trying new things. And I didn't think it was normal to skip a birthday party to go get ice cream with my dad. So I just opened the car door.

"I'll be fine."

He frowned, only reluctantly letting go. "Call me if you want to leave."

"I will."

I went to the front door alone. My throat was so dry I doubted I could talk to anyone even if I wasn't mostly mute.

"I am getting better," I whispered.

I pressed the doorbell and managed a smile when a woman opened it up. She had the same auburn hair and dark eyes and even pale freckles as Erin.

"Sara," she said, "so nice to finally meet you. Come on in."

She waved to my father, and he backed down the driveway very slowly, looking ready to leap out at a moment's notice. Then the door was closed, I could hear voices, and it was too late.

"I'll get Erin," she said. "We are going to do the cake soon. I'll take your coat, dear."

She seemed nice. I was expecting an older chatty Erin, but she spoke slow and soft, and almost seemed shy. I was trying to breathe deeply without her noticing. In through the nose, out through the mouth. My hands were fidgeting nervously at my waist.

"Erin!" she called, starting down the hallway toward the voices.

The move was still clearly in progress. As Erin had promised, there were boxes in the corners, and very few pictures on the walls. There was a family photo, though, and I saw Erin when she was little, full eyebrows and lashes, same lopsided smile. Her father was in a uniform with a beret, standing sternly to the left of the picture, arms rigidly at his side.

I heard footsteps on the stairs and turned to find a man descending. It was him. He was wearing jeans and a T-shirt, but somehow he still looked just as stern as he had in the family photo. His hair was black and cropped short, his face smooth but angled and hard like a statue.

He stopped at the base of the stairs and smiled.

"You're the shy one, right? Sara?"

I nodded.

He extended a hand, and I shook it, forcing a smile. His grip was *very* firm.

"Nice for Erin to have a friend," he said. "It's always tough to move around so much."

It wasn't a question, so I just stared at him, deciding belatedly on another smile.

"You're perfect for her," he continued, sighing. "The girl never stops talking."

"Hey, Sara!"

Erin appeared at his side. She deftly moved around him, grabbed my arm, and pulled me toward the stairs. "I have to show her my room, Dad. Just call us down for the cake. Thanks!"

She pulled me upstairs and into a small bedroom. It too had some unpacked boxes, but the walls were covered with so many posters that I had to search to find a patch of beige paint. The posters ranged from One Direction to *Star Wars* to *Sailor Moon*, all well-worn and crinkled.

"I couldn't decide on a theme," she said, flopping onto the bed. "So I went with pop culture madness. Dad said no more Ryan Gosling shirtless ones. Ugh, my family is exhausting. My brother is so spoiled. It's all 'Kyle, you've grown' and 'how's football going?'"

"I hate football," I murmured.

She sat up. "*Same*. Well, we're going to have to sing to little Mr. Perfect soon, but first I must hear about the park. Was James there? Did you two talk? Did he profess his love for you?"

"No," I said, sitting down at her desk. It was covered in papers and drawings, and I fought the urge to organize it. I wasn't overly neat, but this was chaotic. "Well, yes, yes, and no."

"Rats. What did you talk about?"

"His dead brother."

"Romantic," she said. "But that explains Dr. Ring. Poor guy. Is he crazy like us?"

"I don't think so. He's just grieving."

"Shame," she said. "He could have joined our clique. We could have used a boy."

I was happy he wasn't like us, but I didn't want to say that. I just turned to her desk and looked over the scattered papers. Drawings of battle scenes. Homework. And, of course, a whole lot of stars. She scribbled them into most margins, even on the homework.

She wandered over, picking up one of the drawings. "Terrible, I know. But I spend a stupid amount of time by myself

"*I* do not go to Dr. Ring to be normal," she said. "I go to manage my disorder."

"That's the same as trying to be normal," I insisted.

Of course she wanted to be normal. That was the whole point.

Her eyes flashed. "I thought we agreed we were Star Children."

She went back to the bed to sit down. I didn't understand what I'd done wrong this time. It was fun to pretend to be Star Children. But it was pretend. A placeholder.

But as I turned around and saw Erin holding her sheet of paper, I was suddenly less sure. She was staring down at it. Her eyes looked glassy, and I realized that maybe it was only pretend to me. There really were a lot of printouts on her desk. There were a lot of stars in the margins. Maybe she really did believe in this. Maybe she *needed* to. Was it really my job to ruin that fantasy for her?

I sat down beside her. Pretend or not, I thought the three tenets made a lot of sense.

And tenet number two was that Star Children always help each other.

"We are," I said, taking the sheet from her. "But we can't go telling all the Muggles."

She paused. "We're really mixing source material here."

"Star Children can do what they want," I replied simply. "We are brilliant, after all."

in here, so I need a hobby." She smiled. "What's

I thought about that. "Reading. Writing. Pret
a warrior queen."

"Naturally." She sat down on the desk and look
"So . . . did you hold hands?"

"No!" I said. "He is a friend. Maybe. I don't know.
he is just a park friend."

"What do you mean?"

I hesitated. I thought I had moved on, but maybe I w
quite over it.

"I don't think he really wants to be seen with me."

She was silent for a moment. She can really glare wh
she wants to.

"That's not cool."

I flushed. "Just for now. Once I am a little more normal—"

"*Normal?*" she said, throwing her hands up. "What does
that mean? Did he say that?"

"No, of course not," I said, looking at the door. She was
basically shouting. I lowered my voice. "Normal behavior.
Most people don't understand Sara breaks. They don't know
that I might freak out for no reason." I picked up a drawing.
"They would laugh about Star Children."

Erin took the paper from me, scowling. "That's their
problem."

"It's *our* problem," I corrected her. "We're trying to be
more normal, remember? That's why we go to see Dr. Ring."

She turned and hugged me, giving me a face full of auburn hair that I had to spit out.

"Thanks," she said. "I guess you can have your gift, then."

"What gift?"

She jumped up and retrieved something out of a desk drawer, giggling the whole way. It was a bracelet with little golden charms—stars. It still had a tag on it, but she plucked it off.

"I bought this last week," she said excitedly. "Well, I bought two of them. Wrist."

I stuck my wrist out, and she wrapped it around and clasped it there, grinning.

"Star Child," she whispered. "Let me get mine."

As she went to put on her own, I lifted the bracelet and stared at it, biting my lip and feeling a strange rush of emotion. It was silly. Stupid, even. But no one had ever really given me a gift, except for my mom and dad.

I shook my wrist and let the stars catch the light.

"Well?" she said, showing off her matching bracelet.

"I love it."

"Are you getting teary?" she asked.

"No—"

"Ugh, you are going to make me cry! I love us. We're brilliant and fabulous and hot."

"Erin!" someone called up the stairs. "Cake time!"

She pulled me to my feet and linked arms, turning to the bedroom door.

"Star Children unite," she muttered. "We are going to need it to cope with my family."

Everyone stood in a loose circle around the table, lit by the candles on the cake. Erin's older brother was staring down at it, looking very uninterested in the whole process, and Erin was rolling her eyes while everyone all sang. There were twelve people there aside from me. Some were family, but Erin said most were other soldiers from the base. More than a few of them were looking at me curiously, so I just kept my head down, trying to breathe and pretend no one else was there. But it was a lot of new eyes, and a lot of noise, and I was trying very hard to remember that this was a normal thing. *People sing. People get together sometimes. No one wants to hurt you. No one is watching. You are fine. You are fine.* I could feel little tingles all over my body, like bursts of static electricity.

"How old are you now?" one man took up, extending the song.

I dug my nails into my skin. The wheel was not spinning yet, but it was close. It wasn't going to be Strong Girl. It was False Alarm or Danger Game, and both were going to be very bad. What did Dr. Ring say? Focus on the moment. Be mindful. Find something to be aware of.

I stared at her brother, his finger tapping impatiently on the table. His pent-up sighs.

I imagined him as some petulant prince, bored as his subjects lavished praise on him while his sister plotted to overthrow him. Judging by Erin's face, it was a definite possibility.

The song turned into cheers as he blew out the candles. If I could just tolerate a few more minutes, we would go back to Erin's room and be alone. I could calm down there.

Her brother forced a smile. "Thank you. Great singing."

"It was all me," the man boasted. "I have the voice of an angel."

"Let's get a family picture!" a woman said, taking out her phone.

Erin reluctantly fell in beside her brother, framed by their parents. I could see Erin's discomfort. She was turning a bit from the camera, showing one side, her hands fidgeting . . . probably fighting the urge to hide her face. To pull out something. I tried to smile at her, sensing that she needed help more than me now. I knew what she was feeling. The urges and the voices that seemed to get louder when everyone else did. The realization they were watching.

"Let me get one!" someone else insisted.

Erin tried to step away. "We can share photos. Welcome to the future, people."

"I agree," her brother muttered.

"Stay still," her father said.

His voice seemed to cut over the noise. He wasn't loud, but he didn't need to be.

For some reason, I flinched. So did Erin.

"I don't like getting my picture taken—" Erin said, making her way to me.

His hand was suddenly on her arm. It was so fast I didn't see it until it was sitting there, fingers wrapped around her bicep. He pulled her back, almost imperceptibly, and she opened her mouth for a second, like she was ready to cry out. But she stopped moving and tried to force a smile.

"Okay," she said, stepping back into the photo.

It felt like a long time. She stood there while four or five different people took photos, wearing a smile that I was sure would melt away the second the photos stopped. Her eyes went to me once and then stayed far away. And mine stayed on those strong fingers. Still grasping.

No one else seemed to notice. I felt like there were three of us in the room. Erin, her father hurting her, and me, seeing it but saying nothing and wondering if I could.

When the photos stopped, Erin took two plates of cake and led me back upstairs. She slammed the door behind us and went right to the bed to eat. I followed slowly, watching her.

"Everyone needs a photo," she muttered. "You know how many of them asked me about my eyelashes? 'Oh, your poor lashes! Are you okay? And your eyebrows? What's going on?'"

She dug into the cake, shoving big, crumbly bites into her mouth and talking through it.

"'Nothing, Grandma. I'm just a freak. Thank you for asking.' Now they can all post it and tag me so extended family can comment too. 'Oh, is Erin okay? Boy, that brother is handsome!'"

Her eyes were watering now, and I just sat down next to her.

"We should add another tenet," I said.

She wiped her nose. "What?"

"Never be ashamed of being a Star Child," I said softly.

She laughed, wiping her eyes, and we leaned against each other's shoulders and finished the cake. If nothing else, it was delicious. We stayed up there the rest of the night, talking and laughing and pausing only for her to run down and say good-bye to relatives. It seemed normal.

But when I left, I was thinking about the fingers, and more so, what they had left behind.

CHAPTER 14

GOOD-BYE, MS. HUGGER

Erin and I texted all day Sunday, but I never brought up her father. I wanted to, but I remembered the last time. I was her friend, and it wasn't my job to make her upset. So by the time Monday morning arrived, I had forgotten about the party—other than the fact that I made it through without an incident. Maybe I was getting better.

In the afternoon we went to go choose our book of the week. I love our library time, even if the librarian thinks I am a weirdo. We walked in and Mrs. Yeltson just gave me a suspicious look.

"Something light this week," Ms. Hugger said. "I have plans over the weekend."

I started down the second aisle for the middle grade fiction category, scanning the shelves. Something light . . . Then I heard the library doors swing open, followed by a wave of voices. I snuck a peek through the shelves and saw that a seventh-grade class was coming in.

"Fiddlesticks," I murmured.

"One hour!" their teacher, Mrs. Gregory, said. "And we don't all have to use computers!"

They all used computers except for one: Daniel Leigh. He was with his best friend, Max, at first, as always, but Max sat down with Taj to play a computer game, and Daniel wandered alone into the shelves. He had sandy-blond hair and blue eyes and was nearly as pale as me, despite playing football outside. He had something wrong with him, I was sure. I had seen hints: soft words and sweating and muscles tensing. Something screaming below the surface.

I watched him through a crack in the shelves. He was looking at some adult fiction they kept in the library for teachers and overachievers like us. He was a closet overachiever, though. He was only looking there now because he thought he was alone.

I picked up a book called *The Runaway Robot* by Lester del Rey. I was about one page in when I realized the robot was telling the story. I closed it and tucked both copies under my arm.

When I snuck another peek through the shelves, Daniel was playing a Game. Not one of mine—clearly, Daniel had his own.

He picked up a book and put it back and picked it up.

His body was stiff. I thought I could hear him whispering. He kept looking down the aisle to make sure no one was watching. Maybe he could feel my eyes on him. But his body was shaking, and I could almost feel it when he clenched his fists—a rising pressure that wanted to burst out of his eyeballs and throat and skin.

"Seven, eight, nine, seven, eight, nine," he whispered, and he put it back and picked it up, and then he dug his nails into his scalp so hard I was sure it must have cut him. "Seven, eight, nine, seven, eight, nine, seven, eight, nine . . ."

At each number he put the book back on the shelf, and it seemed like he wanted to keep it there on the ninth, but he couldn't and had to do it seven times, eight times, and then try again. It was eleven more full sequences before he left. And even then, he moved slowly. Reluctantly, looking back once before hurrying away. He hadn't beaten his Game. He was just like me.

I watched him go, and I felt bad for him. But I felt good, too. Relieved.

I now knew for sure that I wasn't the only crazy kid in Erie Hills Public School.

That realization turned to guilt, and that turned to a reminder that *he* wasn't in the Crazy Box. He was stronger than me, or at least a far better actor. The relief turned to jealousy.

That night I read the entire book because I didn't want to

turn off the lights. I had done something bad. Two partially dissolved pills sat on my desk; I had spit them out and shoved them into my pocket as soon as Mom turned around. I didn't want to take them anymore. Things were going well. It had been a good day . . . not even a single Game. But even though I hated taking the pills, I was afraid of what would happen if I didn't. Finally, when the book was done, I turned off the lights and lay there, trying to remind myself that I was getting better.

I wasn't the only one staying up. I had thirteen text messages from Erin, all of the usual variety:

Someone posted a photo from the birthday party. Thanks, Aunt Deb!!

Do you ever wonder why peanut butter isn't called peanut paste?

I think a boy just flirted with me. He said hey, but it was a loaded hey.

But at 10:15, I got one from James. I saw his name and opened it right away.

Hey! It's James. Guess what: I went in my brother's room again. I didn't get a panic attack!

I smiled and wrote back:

You are making progress.

There was a pause.

Maybe. Some days are still bad.

I read that and then stared at the ceiling again, screen

open, bathed in blue light. James had some bad days for now. Then it would be one a week. One a month. Then normal James again. And he would want normal friends. Friends who didn't take pills or play games. I had to change. It felt like I was adding glue, just a little at a time, enough to fix the cracks but never be truly fixed. But I realized I was being selfish. James had lost his brother. He needed support.

You're doing good, I wrote back. Keep going. Good night, James.

James: Good night, Sara.

I turned of the screen and let the darkness come back. It always came back for me.

I slept for about an hour that night, which was not enough. I didn't take my pills and surprise! I played False Alarm twice. And when my mom gave me my morning dose, I took it and tried not to feel like a failure and failed at that too.

I yawned all through math, and blinked through English, and my head started wobbling during science even thought it was my favorite subject.

Finally Ms. Hugger put the textbook away and sat down on the edge of my desk.

"Tired?" she asked dryly.

I blinked. It felt like my eyelids had glue on them. "A little."

"Me too." Ms. Hugger sighed. "Sara, I have to tell you something."

"Okay."

"I will be leaving at the end of the semester."

I looked at her, awake now. "Where are you going?"

"I will be working with a student at another school. A boy with autism."

I thought about that for a moment. It didn't make sense. We got along. We liked each other. Or . . . I liked her. I racked my brain for all the times I had annoyed her. There were a lot.

"Did I make you leave?" I murmured.

"No! Of course not. Working with autism is just my specialty, and the school thought I was the best candidate for him. He's been struggling. Someone new will be taking over for me."

"Oh."

I kept my eyes on the desk.

She squeezed my hand. "Do you want to talk about it?"

"No."

"Sara—"

I pulled my hand away and started drawing a blue whale. I had been working on them.

"You're going to have someone great take over, trust me," Ms. Hugger said.

"Okay."

"We still have a little while together."

"Why?" I said softly. "Just leave now."

I drew a big tail fin and the water passing beneath it. She was swimming fast.

"Sara, this isn't because of you. You will be fine with a new teacher—"

"You said I wasn't getting better," I whispered. "You told me that."

"It's not always about *getting better*—"

"Yes, it is!" I shrieked.

That wasn't her job. I knew that. But I didn't want her to go.

Her eyes were glassy now. "Sara, we have still made a lot of progress—"

I drew more wavy lines around the whale, her tail pointed at me. She was going faster and faster now, swimming away from Psycho Sara. Why wouldn't she? Everyone should. Maybe everyone would eventually.

"I hate it here!" I screamed. "I hate this room! I hate you!"

I ripped up my drawing and I scattered the floor with whale parts. I started to cry. Ms. Hugger hugged me. I think she was crying too.

We did that for a while, and then we picked up the scraps of paper together and had lunch. I could tell that she was sad. Her eyes were still glassy, and she ate slowly. I put my sandwich down, taking a deep breath. I may be crazy, but I am not cruel.

"Ms. Hugger?" I said.

"Yes, Sara?"

"I think you are a very good teacher."

She smiled and bit her lip. "Thank you, Sara."

We went back to our lunches. I was in control again. I needed to be smarter. Everyone else had given up on fixing me, but not *me*. I just had to follow my rules and focus.

You will be better soon.

CHAPTER 15

I SEE STARS

On Wednesday I asked if we could eat lunch in the cafeteria. Ms. Hugger clearly still felt bad about leaving at the end of the semester, so she said yes right away.

We always get to sit alone . . . even if someone was at the table before we sat down. Ms. Hugger was eating an apple and reading, so I just ate in silence and people-watched.

"I think they found my replacement for next semester," Ms. Hugger said suddenly.

"Who?" I asked.

I'd had three special education teachers in my life and seriously hated two of them.

"Miss Lecky. Principal Surrin says she is highly recommended."

"Super."

She lowered her phone. "I know that change is hard. But you'll like her."

"I liked you." I didn't mean for it to sound so accusatory.

She put her book down altogether and sighed. "I don't want you to think that—"

And then something hard connected with the back of my skull.

My head snapped to the side. and I saw stars and heard screaming and Ms. Hugger was yelling at a boy named Brian who looked completely horrified. The stars cleared and I felt a sharp, shooting pain and something warm in my hair. I touched my head and found blood.

"We were playing around," Brian said, almost pleading. "I got pushed. We were just getting pumped up for the game. I didn't see you guys, I promise. Oh man, I am so, so sorry."

He was almost in tears, but I think Ms. Hugger had been waiting for a chance to yell.

"Get to the office! Now!" she shrieked. The whole cafeteria was looking. "Now!"

Ms. Hugger pressed a napkin to my head and led me to the office while Brian shuffled along behind us. She burst through the door and everything went mad.

"He punched her!" Ms. Hugger screamed. "Band-Aids!"

The receptionist dropped her phone. Principal Surrin

came flying out of her office. Even the little kid waiting on one of the chairs went white.

"I got pushed!" Brian pleaded. "I didn't punch her! It was just my elbow—"

Principal Surrin stared at us in disbelief. "Brian . . . my office . . . now," she whispered.

Brian went in like a lamb to slaughter while I was led to the nurse's office. Ms. Hugger was completely manic. She was pacing and checking my scalp as the nurse held gauze to my head. I half expected an MRI.

I knew I was getting the crazy girl treatment. *Don't punch Sara in the head, silly Brian. You might knock another screw loose!* I hoped he put one back in place.

"Your mother didn't answer, but your father is on his way," Principal Surrin said, coming into the room.

Uh-oh.

"Do you feel dizzy?" Ms. Hugger asked. "How many fingers am I holding up?"

It was two, but I didn't feel I should dignify that with an answer.

"It's just a cut," the receptionist said. "It might need a few stitches."

I was hoping she was wrong about the stitches. I hated the hospital.

Fifteen minutes later, Dad came in. I was surprised he didn't shatter the glass door. He was wearing his orange town jacket and his eyes were wild. I was back in the waiting room with an ice pack squeezed to my head, and I turned to him, grimacing. Ms. Hugger jumped to her feet.

"Mr. Malvern—"

"Who hurt my daughter?" he hissed.

"He's being dealt with—" Ms. Hugger said.

"*Who?*" he snapped.

I had never seen him so angry. His whole body was shaking.

Ms. Hugger could see the danger now. "A boy. It was an accident—"

"You don't hit people by accident," he said. "Where is he?"

Principal Surrin walked out and put on her most serious voice. "Mr. Malvern, correct?"

He looked at her and she halted midstep. She probably saw his eyes. Then she stepped in front of the door to her office, where poor Brian was probably hiding under a desk. My father started that way with fists clenched and murder on his face. Even Principal Surrin looked afraid.

I was up instantly. I wrapped him up in a hug, letting my ice pack fall. I hugged him so tightly that he had to stop walking or drag me with him. His body was tense, shaking, but then he seemed to notice me and stopped. He bent down and softly ran his fingers over the Band-Aid.

He cupped my face and looked at me. "You okay?"

I nodded.

"She . . . she could maybe use a few stitches," the receptionist offered meekly.

He breathed for a moment, considering. I think he still wanted to kill Brian.

I looked at him and mouthed, "Can we go?"

He nodded. "Okay."

Then he took my hand and led me out in silence.

CHAPTER 16

AN UNCOMFORTABLE
MEETING AND ICE CREAM

He decided I had to get stitches. That meant more strangers, more waiting, and angrier Daddy as he watched me flinch while the doctor sewed me up like a doll. I could hear his teeth grinding. When we finally got home, we watched TV and ate ice cream. Mom was already home when we got there. She was on the phone with the principal for a while and then announced that both sets of parents were going to attend an apology meeting tomorrow. Dad muttered something threatening. I wasn't thrilled about the plan either.

She also called Dr. Ring's office to let him know that I wouldn't be attending that night. Erin naturally texted me immediately after the session to see where I was, and I replied that I was punched in the head. That was probably unwise. She sent four text messages and then called, and I had to explain everything. She offered to personally beat up Brian for me, but I told her she would have to get in line. My dad seemed unwilling to let me out of his sight. He was also cracking his knuckles a lot.

"You all right?" I asked him.

He grunted. "Fine. You know, I could just give him one good right—"

"No punching children," my mom said, walking by on her way to the kitchen.

He grunted again and turned to me, checking my head. "How does it feel—"

"Same as ten minutes ago," I said. "I'm fine. I can take a punch. I'm like Rocky."

He snorted and pulled me in under his arm. "That you can. It's what I admire most."

"That I can take a punch?"

"Yeah. You go through a lot."

I frowned. "I don't think—"

He turned my chin to face him. "You're the strongest person I know. Stronger than me, that's for sure. But if that boy ever looks at you again, I will turn him into some sort of paste."

I giggled. "We're going to see him tomorrow."

"He gets a pass for the apology."

He pulled me in tighter, and I thought about what he said.

* * *

The next day, Brian and I were sandwiched between our respective sets of parents.

"Go ahead," Brian's mother said. Her hands clearly still wanted to smack him.

"I am very, very sorry," Brian said. "It was an accident, but it was stupid. I'm sorry."

Principal Surrin was at the head of the oval table wearing a pantsuit, which she probably only wore for serious occasions. I had been in the office boardroom before, but I had never gotten a pantsuit. She turned to my parents.

"And on behalf of the school, we sincerely apologize that this event occurred as well."

"Not your fault," my mother said. She gave Brian a friendly smile. "Accidents happen."

My father was like a statue. He didn't smile or flinch. Brian's parents watched him nervously. They had probably heard that he wanted to murder their child yesterday and twenty-four hours wasn't really sufficient for a cooldown. Brian's father looked ready to make a block.

"I am very sorry," Brian said again, and this time he looked at me.

I nodded. He really was sorry. Even for bullies, punching the crazy girl is low.

"Brian will be much more careful about roughhousing in the future," his mother said.

She laid a hand on his shoulder and must have squeezed because he nodded hastily.

"Good," my mom replied. "Well, I think we can all move on."

Principal Surrin shifted. Her eyes were on my father. I knew this was for him.

"We're . . . *all* okay with moving on?" she asked.

My father managed a curt nod, and Brian and his family quickly left the room.

"He seems like a nice boy," my mother said. "No harm done."

"Except for three stitches," my father replied coolly.

My mother rolled her eyes. "Sara is fine. Thank you, Principal Surrin. I should get back to work. Sara can get back to class—"

"I already took the day off," my dad said. "I'm going to take Sara home."

"Of course," Principal Surrin said. "I'll tell Ms. Hugger."

My mom glanced at my dad. "Are you sure—"

"Yes."

And that was final. Even Principal Surrin knew it because she stood up and ushered us to the door. We walked out of the school as a family—Mom and Dad and me in between them.

"Can we get ice cream?" I asked.

We had already gotten some last night, but I figured it was worth a shot.

"Yes," my father said.

"No," my mother said.

They looked at each other, and then my mother relented. "Just a quick stop, then."

Ten minutes later we were sitting in Dairy Queen. My mother was being thoroughly trounced in passive-aggressive arguments today, probably because my father still looked a bit murderous. We sat at a square table, Daddy and me eating Blizzards while my mother drank ice water.

My father was watching her sip on it and seemed even angrier, but I wasn't sure why.

"What are you and Sara going to do today?" my mother asked.

"Hang out," my father said.

"Hmm," she replied.

She looked at her cell phone, obviously impatient.

But I loved Oreo Blizzards. I was savoring it. And then my dad sat up straighter.

"Your friend from work is here," he said to my mom.

I followed his gaze and saw a man waiting at the counter. He was big and broad and had red tattoos on his forearm. Dad said he was a friend from Mom's work, but he was wearing overalls and had work gloves in his back pocket. That did not seem like normal attire for an insurance office. My mother looked and my father looked, and the man stiffened when he saw my dad.

"Oh . . . yes," my mother said.

"Call him over," my father said. "John, right?"

John waved and smiled a fake smile and ordered a cone.

"He's going to leave soon," my father continued calmly.

My mother waved and said hello, but her back was rigid. And that was all I needed. The roses and the fighting. It all fit together now.

A lot of things went through my head. My parents were going to get a divorce. Where was I going to go? What would my dad do? Why would my mom do this to us? Was it my fault?

John walked over to us, but he clearly didn't want to. "Ice cream break?" he said.

"Yeah," my mother said in a small voice.

"You?" my father asked.

"Yeah," he said. "Just on a break."

He seemed to think about that, and my father just smiled and said, "Where do you work?"

John paused, but he probably knew he was beaten. "The car plant. I'm on the line."

"Ah," my father said. "Good pay there, I hear. Nice pension."

"Pretty good, yeah," he replied quietly. "Well, I won't keep you guys. Enjoy."

"Bye now," my father replied. My mother nodded and went back to her water.

I didn't say anything. I just ate my ice cream and nobody spoke anymore.

That night I lay down in bed. I was finishing up *Harry Potter and the Sorcerer's Stone* for the eleventh time because I wanted to remember that people can look normal even when they're not.

> "The truth." Dumbledore sighed. "It is a beautiful and terrible thing, and should therefore be treated with great caution."

My door was open and my parents were talking. Well, yelling.

"It's always my fault, isn't it?" my mother said.

"Of course it's your fault! Who else?"

"It takes two!"

"Or three!"

"You drove me to this!"

"Keep your voice down!"

"Like she doesn't know."

"She doesn't need to know anything else."

There was a hard laugh. "She knows just about everything around here. You know that."

"Not everything."

"And whose fault is that?" he said.

"Oh, I forgot," she replied. "Everything is my fault."

"When was it? When did you decide to stop trying?"

"A long time after you did," she snapped.

There was silence for a moment.

"How long can we go on like this?" my mother asked.

"Why don't you ask your date tomorrow?"

"How dare you. Where are you going?"

"Out for a while," my father said.

The door slammed and it was very quiet.

I read on, because that's all there was to do, and stopped at a different line:

If there is one thing Voldemort cannot understand, it is love.

"That makes two of us," I murmured.

CHAPTER 17

PIRATES

The weekend went by quickly. Lots of reading and ice on the head and reflecting on whether or not that counted as my first fight and if I was basically now a warrior queen. I decided yes.

On Monday, Ms. Hugger and I just went right back to our routine and didn't talk about her leaving or getting punched. I had one round of False Alarm in the morning, but Ms. Hugger just said it was "understandable" and gave me some extra quiet time. We stayed in the Crazy Box for lunch, though, even on Tuesday and Wednesday. I was back in solitary confinement.

I still didn't say anything to Mom and Dad about John. I decided to pretend I didn't know anything. Maybe I didn't. My parents were staying together. They loved each other. Period.

I still wasn't very good at lying, especially to myself. But for this, I wanted to try.

On Thursday my mom woke me up and went to make breakfast. Mornings were supposed to be a "finely tuned machine," according to her, but it was more like a dance. Daddy was long gone to work, so it was just us, and we sort of circled around each other, always a few minutes behind the other one. She ate breakfast first; I showered first. She went to check emails after that, and I brushed my teeth. She showered; I packed up my homework. We didn't talk or interact, except when it was time for me to take my pills.

The day went by okay. Ms. Hugger and I still didn't talk about the fact that she was leaving. There was no memo or anything, but it seemed like a good idea. And the day was just math and geography and reading right until I was sitting in group therapy. Erin was sitting close enough that our shoulders were touching.

"Who punches people?" she asked incredulously. "Boys are the worst."

"I'm right here," Peter grumbled.

"Case in point," she replied.

Dr. Ring sat down and opened his notebook, looking around the circle.

"How was your week, Peter? Anything to discuss?"

"It always comes to me first," Peter muttered. "I wish I was mute like Sara."

and a woman as well, wearing a torn—yet surprisingly clean—dress.

"Is this what romance is supposed to look like?" I asked.

"I guess so. Maybe less abs."

"Pirates are also technically murderers and thieves," I pointed out.

She waved a hand as we pulled out onto the road. "Irrelevant."

"How do you know if . . ."

I bit my lip. *Don't do it. Don't do it.* I did it.

"If you like someone?" I finished.

I think she almost drove us off the road, but she recovered quickly. "James?"

"Unnamed," I corrected. "This is theoretical only. Muscular pirate."

She nodded. "Well, first, you are twelve. So the obvious answer is no you don't like anyone ever and please don't tell your father or he will kill the boy. Second, you just know."

"Oh."

She reached out and squeezed my hand. "You went from no real friends to two fast. Of course you are going to be confused. For now, for *years*, a friend is what you need. Trust me. But it's okay to have a crush. Lots of people get them around your age. It's a completely normal thing."

A normal thing. Excellent. I could add it to my rules.

I set the book down, wondering how the lady kept her

"So do we," Erin said.

"That will do," Dr. Ring cut in, frowning. "We can come back to you. Erin?"

"No issues."

"Mel—"

She was already shaking her head. Taisha wasn't there this week, and Dr. Ring didn't even bother with me. He just sighed and put his pen down, his eyes pausing on my Band-Aid.

"Right," Dr. Ring said. "We aren't talkative this week, I see. Well, that says more than you might think. Why don't we discuss silence as a coping strategy?" He gave me a knowing look. "Our voice is how we project our thoughts. But if we don't trust our thoughts, we don't trust ourselves to speak them. We are afraid of making mistakes. Of being vulnerable. Vulnerability is human . . . but it's also scary. We want to be untouchable."

I didn't meet his eyes. Dr. Ring had discussed this with me many times before. I protected myself by not speaking. I tried to keep control.

Of course I wanted control. Half the time I felt like I didn't have *any*. My parents fed me emotions in a bottle. For all I knew, the pills were making me this version of Sara. Who could blame me for trying to take whatever control I could get?

"Of course," Dr. Ring continued, "the problem when we

dress so clean, and who had so neatly sliced it from her shoulder to the top of a lace corset. A master swordfighter, I presumed. She was looking at him with wide eyes, which could have been love or the realization that she was probably about to be murdered and thrown overboard. Maybe it was the same expression.

I looked at Mom. I had to ask, even if I knew. "Do you still love Daddy?"

Her smile went tight, like a line drawn on with a marker. "Of course. We're just . . ."

"Fighting a lot?"

"Exactly," she said. "Sometimes people fight. It doesn't change the way they feel."

I nodded. She was saying what I wanted to hear, but I guess that was her job. She was right about James, though. A friend was nice. It was all I needed. Nice, normal friends.

But we drove home and I stared at the book cover and thought about James anyway.

NOTE (ON PIRATES)

Yes, I may have taken the book when my mother wasn't looking. Yes, I may have read the whole thing. Yes, I may have occasionally found it sweet despite the constant threats of murder.

And what I learned is this: Even if I ripped James's corset, he couldn't just hang around with a pirate. He either had to become a pirate, or I had to become something normal. A cobbler, maybe. I had to become normal, and I had to hurry up.

Oh, and don't fall in love with a real pirate. The book may have left it out, but historically, pirate hygiene was simply awful.

"I think it would be nice if we *all* celebrated your promotion."

She hesitated and my father nodded.

"Maybe next time," he said quietly.

"Yeah," she replied. "Maybe next time. We are all due for a night out."

My father picked up his half-eaten dinner and went to the kitchen, and I heard him dump it all out into the garbage. My mother and I ate in silence.

I went to the park the next day, but James wasn't there. I waited for two hours in the cold and then went home disappointed. I knew his last name was Bennett from the contact he put in my phone, and I had looked him up and found an address the same day. I wrote it down and tucked it away, telling myself it was just for emergencies.

Obviously, I couldn't just go to his house. Could I?

No. Of course not.

This was all very confusing. I had never had a crush. Well, not on a real person. I'd had lots of fictional crushes, mostly the sad and forlorn: Severus Snape, Sydney Carton, even Piggy.

But this was new. It was weird, illogical behavior. Why did I look up his address? Why did I go to the park today even though it was cold and damp? Why was I staring at my rules for being normal and reading the same rule about James over and over like it was the only one?

I sat on my bed and toyed with the Star Child bracelet. I only wore it when I was seeing Erin, and mostly I just kept it in a drawer. A month ago, I was Psycho Sara. I hated her, but I understood her. Quiet. Afraid. Reclusive. Now I had made a friend, and had a crush, and things were confusing. I could hardly keep up. But it was good. It had to be, right?

I slipped off the bracelet and tucked it back in the drawer. I really was grateful for the gift. But I didn't need more made-up words and excuses to be different. I had enough of those.

My dad was on the couch downstairs, surrounded by a little garden of beer bottles. He patted the spot beside him when he saw me, throwing a heavy, sagging arm around my shoulders.

"Come to watch some football?" he said.

"You know that I hate football."

He laughed. "Excited for the movies tonight? You know, you only used to go with me."

"I'm too cool for that now," I replied, leaning into his chest.

"I knew the day would come." He took a deep swig of beer. "Will James be there?"

"No," I said quickly. "Just Erin and me."

"Hmm. Should we talk about boys? I.e., how I will kill any of them that come near you?"

"Mom talks too much," I muttered.

"You're twelve," he said. "No dating until you are forty. Not a day earlier."

"Seems extreme."

"I thought fifty was unreasonable." He sighed. "We are proud of you, Princess."

I glanced at him. "For what?"

"For doing this group therapy. For making a friend."

"I think making a friend is pretty commonplace."

"For some," he agreed. "But we all get to set our own goalposts."

I groaned. "You ruined it with the football reference."

He pulled me in and gave me a noogie until I was laughing and trying to get away. I ended up under his arm again, hair everywhere, exhausted, face wet from the tears.

"You know, you can't noogie me now that I'm cooler than you," I muttered.

"If anything, I think I have to do it more. Make sure you don't get a big head."

I laughed. "Daddy?"

"Yeah?"

I was supposed to pretend. I was going to. But . . . I had to be ready. Just in case.

"Are you and Mom getting a divorce?"

He was quiet for a moment. "No. It's just a bad time. Don't you worry about it."

"I'm not stupid."

He snorted. "If anything, you are too smart for your own good. We're fine."

When you want to believe something, it's easier to pretend. I smiled and stood up.

"I'm going to go do anything in the world except watch football."

"You know, you might like it one day. Some girls fall for football players."

I grunted and started for the kitchen. "I can assure you that I will *never* be one of them."

Erin's mom dropped us off in front of the theater. I had spent most of the car ride wondering where Erin had gotten her chattiness. It certainly wasn't from her dad. Erin talked the whole way about school and boys and her outfit—she was wearing jeans and a new pink sweater—and about how much popcorn she was going to eat. My dad had given me twenty dollars. I hoped it was going to be enough.

"You sure your mother is okay to come get you later?" Erin's mom asked.

I nodded, and she drove off without another word. Erin grabbed my arm and started for the entrance, practically skipping along. She had her hair curled and done up, eyebrows drawn on. She hadn't been able to come over an hour early, since her mom wanted to drive us there and not home, so only she had any makeup on. I was just wearing a hoodie with my hair in a ponytail.

"I haven't been out with a friend in, like, two years," she said. "This is awesome. I'm going to eat ten bags of popcorn. I bet there will be cute boys everywhere. How do I look?"

"Nice."

"*Nice?*"

I paused. "Beautiful? Transcendent? Radiant—"

"Thank you," she said, giving me a queenly nod. "You may continue once we sit down."

The lobby was busy. There were a lot of kids, some close to our age and most older, and I felt my breathing go shallow as we picked our way to ticket machines.

As Erin bought tickets, I glanced around, my skin prickling. So many people and eyes and voices and all of them strangers. Maybe this was a bad idea. We could still head home.

I felt Erin's hand slip over mine.

"Come on," she said. "I already got your ticket."

She led me to the snack counter, and I gave her my twenty. She got us two drinks and two popcorns and quickly led us toward the theater. She kept shooting me reassuring looks, shifting her fingers on mine, clammy as they were. I was reprimanding myself. This was stupid. I shouldn't have come. I was going to have a freak-out and everyone was going to stare and—

"Let's just get seated," Erin whispered, pulling me into the darkness.

We found seats near the back, in the corner, and she turned to me.

"You're doing great. We're in now."

"I don't know—"

She squeezed my hand and turned to me. "Just try. If you need to go, we'll leave."

I nodded, taking a deep breath. She was right. We were tucked away in the corner now, in a dark theater, where no one was supposed to talk anyway. I focused on Erin's voice, making sure I nodded and smiled and did all the right things to show my brain we could relax. I could almost hear Dr. Ring: *Ground yourself. Breathe. Don't drift. Stay focused.*

The lights dimmed, the previews started, and I focused on the movie. It was a romantic comedy, and not very good, but Erin laughed and we spilled popcorn and I didn't panic once.

When the lights came on, I was still in my seat. A sense of relief swept over me. Pride, even. I had gone out to a movie theater. No breaks. No calls home. Not a single panic attack.

Erin sighed and stretched, yawning. "What did you think?"

"Good," I said. "It was really good."

"No, it wasn't," she replied, laughing. "But I know what you mean."

I noticed that some of her makeup had smeared. One of her eyebrows was mostly gone. I kept quiet.

We were leaving, and I didn't want to upset her.

We filed out at the tail end of the crowd, and I sent a text to my mom to come pick us up. We made our way to the front doors of the lobby and waited there. It was late November and the temperature had dropped sharply.

Of course, everyone else who needed a ride was waiting there too. It was busy and loud, and most of the people there were groups of kids like us, all bunched into little, noisy circles. A group of older boys was standing a few feet away. One of them looked over at us.

"Ugh, does every boy have to look at you?" Erin said, grinning.

I had quickly looked away. He went to my school. An eighth grader named Kevin. The others went to my school too. They knew about me. I tensed, stomach clenching right up again.

"Of course, they may be taking in my perfect eyebrows," she added.

She touched them subconsciously, and I hoped we could leave soon. Then I heard the laughter. I tried not to listen.

"Psycho Sara is here?" one of them was saying. "And she has a friend!"

"I got to take a picture."

"Think she talks to her?"

I decided we could deal with a bit of cold. But it was too late. Erin was watching now.

"Are they talking about you?" she asked quietly.

"No," I whispered. "Let's go."

"We need to get her face in the photo," one of the boys said. "Psst . . . Sara—"

Erin stepped toward them, hands planted on her hips. "Can we help you?"

They burst out laughing. I felt my insides curling up. Her eyebrows. The makeup.

"Her face is falling off," Kevin said, snorting.

Erin flushed a brilliant red, her hands going to her eyebrows. "What are you—"

I grabbed her arm to go. I couldn't talk. Not with them watching and laughing.

But she was already feeling her face, her fingers brushing over her last few eyelashes.

"They're both nuts," Kevin muttered.

"Quiet, man—" one of his friends said, even though he was laughing.

"I'm just saying—"

"Saying what?" Erin shouted. She took another step toward them. "Go ahead!"

Everyone was looking at us now. My throat seized up.

"Nothing," Kevin said, waving her away. "Go hang out with Psycho Sara, freak."

"Stop calling her that!" Erin snapped.

"You're missing a spot," a boy said, tapping his eyebrow. "Got a pen?"

I tried to grab Erin's hand. The wheel was spinning fast now. A Game was coming.

But Erin just folded her arms and glared at them.

"Sorry if it offends you," she snarled. "I will remember that next time I get ready."

One of the boys had the decency to blush. The others didn't.

"You got cancer?" Kevin asked.

"No, I don't have cancer," she snapped. "I have a disorder. And stupid people don't help."

I could feel my heart pounding now. I put my finger to my pulse. False Alarm for sure. My breath was short, stomach clenched, skin fiery. I could feel myself drifting away. Maybe it was real this time. Maybe it wasn't a False Alarm. Maybe I really was dying this time. This is how it always went. I always forgot why I called it False Alarm when the panic started. My heartbeat was going much faster now.

"Leave her, man," one of the boys said. "She's nuts."

"I am nuts!" Erin shouted. "We both are! Happy? At least we're not jerks!"

"You do belong with Psycho Sara," Kevin said.

The words started echoing around in my skull. *Psycho psycho psycho.* Why was I here?

I could feel the sweat beading now and tears forming. I had to leave. Otherwise I might just curl up on the spot or scream or maybe die right here, and my daddy would find me, and and and . . . I went for the glass doors. I had to get out. I didn't say anything to Erin. I just ran.

"Sara!" Erin shouted.

I could hear the laughing as she chased after me. I kept running. I didn't know where I was going. Anywhere but here.

"Sara!" Erin caught me by the curb, looking around for my father's car. "Hey!"

"Why did you do that?" I demanded, hand at my neck, trying to count my pulse.

It was so fast. Too fast. Heart attack. No. Relax. Just a panic attack.

"What?"

"Make a scene! Tell them we're . . . we're crazy. We could have just gone somewhere else."

She frowned. "They were insulting us. I could have used backup, if anything."

Erin turned away, muttered something to herself, and then turned back.

"No, I'm sorry . . . I know you don't talk in public," she said. "I'm just all worked up right now. Hey, are you all right?"

She tried to grab at my arm, but I wrenched it away, falling down into a crouch.

"No," I managed, gasping. "I can't breathe."

"It's a panic attack. Just take it easy—"

"We were doing good," I said, my eyes watering. "We were so close."

"To what?" she asked, crouching down beside me.

"A normal night."

She snorted. "Normal. I forgot your big goal. Being normal. Whatever that means."

"Not this!" I said, and pressed my finger to my neck, counting heartbeats. Too fast.

She grabbed my arm. "We are not *normal*."

I pulled away, trying to breathe through my nose, trying to think of something happy, trying not to feel the weights that were suddenly strapped to my arms and legs, pulling me down.

"I am trying," I said.

"And it's going great," Erin said. "Really. 'Cause it's normal to not have eyebrows and eyelashes because I pull them out every time they grow. It's normal that I cry in the mirror every morning and swear I won't do it again but I do *every single time*. We are Star Children, Sara—"

"There's no such thing as Star Children!" I snapped. "It's a game. Make-believe!"

I was talking, but my brain was screaming, "I want to go home! I don't want to die here!" and it all seemed so loud. There were cars pulling up, kids coming out, and I fell silent. That was smarter. Speaking had taken me here. Out of my shell before I was ready. And now I was dying.

"It's about us being special," Erin said quietly. "It's not a game."

I lowered my voice to a whisper. "It's about us lying to our-selves. We have real issues, and we're not helping each other by pretending we don't. I just want to be better. Normal—"

"Stop saying *normal!*" she shrieked. "What does that mean? Huh? What is normal?"

My eyes flooded with tears. "Like everyone else here. You know what I mean."

"Not like me?" Erin said. "Is that it? More like James?"

I wiped my face. I didn't want my dad to see me crying. I just had to breathe.

"I just want to get better."

She stood up. "And that means you don't need Star Chil-dren around, I guess? Huh?"

"No," I said, taking deep breaths, trying to slow down my heart. "Maybe I don't."

Erin stared at me for a moment, nodded, then wiped her eyes. We waited there like that. She stood and looked at noth-ing, and I crouched until my heart started to slow.

The ride home was quiet, and my dad stopped trying to talk after a while. Erin said nothing when we dropped her off, besides "Thank you, Mr. Malvern."

Then she was gone, and when we got home, I said I was tired and no, nothing was wrong, and I sat on my bed and panicked again.

When it passed, I was too tired to brush my teeth. I just lay in bed with my clothes on, pulling the blanket over me.

I had no texts. No missed calls. I was too tired and angry to write one either. Tired of being sick, and angry about it too. Angry that no matter what, the sickness always came back.

I didn't want to make Erin upset, but maybe it was for the best. I didn't need stars. I needed normal.

Tomorrow, I will be better, I told myself. *Tomorrow.*

CHAPTER 19

THE QUEST FOR NORMAL

Sunday was bad. The wheel was spinning all day. Two False Alarms. One Danger Game when I went to the grocery store with my mom. Strong Girl all alone in my room. It felt like a week all in one day, and Erin's words repeated in my mind: *Stop saying* normal! *What does that mean? Huh? What is normal?*

Not this, I thought as I wretched into a toilet. Or when I lay curled into a ball on my bedroom floor, trying to breathe, wondering if I should call for help. Or when the weights got so heavy I couldn't move.

I had taken my medication. Sometimes, it just wasn't enough.

I was happy for Monday. I wasn't sure I was ready to leave the house, but schoolwork was a good distraction, and Ms. Hugger always made me feel better. As soon as she saw me, she decided we should play word games and go pick a new book for the week. It was all supposed to make me feel better. Relax me. Still, she had to give me an extra-long break in the morning, waiting as the panic attack passed.

I saw Kevin and his friends at recess, but they just laughed and stayed far away.

I decided I needed something new to focus on. I found him standing alone by the basketball court, counting. Daniel's friends were all playing, but I gathered he wasn't very good—he seemed to be the substitute most of the time. Like, every recess.

I was supposed to be avoiding crazy people, but he was so good at hiding it—from most people, anyway. I was fascinated. Maybe I could learn something. So I started to watch him.

I began to notice a few important details. One was that he was in love with Raya Singh. That was easy to figure out. He stared at her in the yard, he stared at her at lunch, he stared at her from the bookshelves. So that was one.

He was also very shy around everyone but his best friend, Max. I could relate there.

And most importantly, he kept his craziness a secret. Like a life-or-death kind of secret.

He counted steps in the hallways. It was so obvious, but somehow no one else noticed. He mouthed things to himself when he opened his locker. When he played basketball at recess, he wouldn't step on lines, and sometimes he stepped forward and back for no reason. It was no wonder he wasn't very good. He spaced out bad.

But only if you watched him.

Obsessive-compulsive disorder. I wondered if he knew.

I realized that seeing him suffer made me feel better. I instantly felt guilty. He was trying to keep a secret, and here I was spying on him. I told myself that I would not watch him anymore.

But I knew I would miss it. Because seeing him suffer made me feel less alone.

After school, I was lying in bed reading when my phone buzzed. I snapped it up.

Park?

James. I had thought about texting him a thousand times, but couldn't find the courage. Now I grinned and said **Sure!** and we agreed to meet in twenty minutes.

I was out the door in ten.

I got there first and waited, leaning against the slide. It was cold, and the park was empty, so there was no need to wait out in the grass. I was nervous, but I was also excited. He still wanted to hang out. Maybe he hadn't heard about the movies. Maybe he didn't care. Maybe he liked me.

He showed up soon after, waving as he came close. I smiled. He wasn't wearing plaid today. Not even underneath.

Just a T-shirt and a jacket. His hair was growing back in again.

"Maybe we should walk?" he suggested. "It's colder than I thought."

"Yeah."

We started down the paved path that wove through the park and out into another block of houses. The trees were all bare now, the leaves ground to brown mush or gone right back into the dirt.

"Are we going to discuss the obvious?" I asked.

He frowned, and I stared at his shirt. "Oh. Yeah. Stopped wearing them last week."

"You're really making progress."

"I think so."

"And your mom?"

"We're getting better."

He looked up at the sky and smiled. I followed his gaze. He was probably seeing stars.

"You really helped me," he said.

I looked at him. "What?"

"You did. I always thought of what you said when it got bad. I tried to be calm like you."

I didn't know what to say to that, but he kept looking at me. He needed a response.

"I'm glad I could help," I said.

He glanced at me. "So we can keep doing this?"

"What?"

"Going for walks. Hanging out."

This time, I couldn't hold the smile back. "Yeah. Sure. If you want."

"I do. And thank you. That's what I was trying to say earlier. Thank you."

He reached out and squeezed my hand. It sent tingles up my arm.

"You're welcome," I managed.

But for a moment, I felt sad, too, because it sounded like he didn't need my help anymore.

We walked for a while. The sun was starting to get low, and it got colder.

"We should probably get going," James said at last.

"Yeah."

He walked me to my door, said good night, and started home. I went in smiling.

I didn't like hurting Erin, but I had been right. I needed normal. I needed to start again. I went to my desk and crumpled up the Star Child tenets and put them aside. I took out my notebook instead.

For the next hour I read the rules and wondered if I would need them for much longer.

CHAPTER 20

BETTER YET

On Thursday night I was back in group therapy. Erin came in after me. She refused to look in my direction, sat down diagonally from me, and crossed her arms. I just stared at the floor. Peter was looking between us, and I could see Dr. Ring taking it in as well, frowning.

"Welcome," he said, tapping his pen on his notepad. He cleared his throat. "Does anyone have anything in particular they want to discuss? Erin?"

"Nah," she said.

He paused. "Are you sure?"

"Well, just that some people are jerks and you can't trust anyone including or maybe especially friends."

"I see," Dr. Ring said, glancing at me. "Well, we can talk about that—"

"No need," she cut in. "I have it all figured out. Ignore everyone."

"That's what I've been saying for months," Peter agreed.

Dr. Ring sighed. "We all know that is not an effective strategy. Erin, why do you—"

"Ask *Sara*," she said. She almost spat my name out.

Everyone turned to me. I just fixed my eyes on the floor and said nothing.

"How are we supposed to do that?" Peter said. "She's a mute."

"She's just very *selective*," Erin replied. "Apparently, we aren't good enough."

"Figures," Peter muttered.

No one spoke for a moment. I glanced up and saw Erin pluck her eyelash out. Mel was taking deep breaths, Peter was staring into space, and Taisha was clearly embarrassed. Dr. Ring was taking notes.

I felt my lungs getting heavy like they were full of lead. Not again.

This wasn't supposed to happen anymore.

But the wheel was spinning and the tide was coming and good-bye, Sara Malvern.

I wanted to disappear. So I did.

I left the room and ran to the bathroom. I fell on my knees in front of the toilet and wretched on air and felt tears streaming down my face. Not again. I was breaking the rules.

Finally the door clicked open and Dr. Ring's calm voice came through:

"Breathe, Sara. It will pass."

He came in and stood by the door, blocking the view from anyone else. The pathetic view of a girl choking on air. I stared down at the still water in the toilet. I breathed.

And then my brain said, "Sorry, team. False Alarm. You can all go back to work."

"I'm okay," I croaked. "I'll come back in a second."

Dr. Ring nodded and closed the door behind him. When I came out, Erin was waiting.

"You okay?" she asked stiffly.

I nodded, and then she did the same and stormed back in to join the group.

Dr. Ring stepped out. "Do you want to talk?"

"I . . . I think I am going to go home," I said.

He nodded. "Of course." He laid a hand on my arm. "Fighting is a part of friendship."

"I don't have any friends," I said, and then hurried outside to the van.

My mom frowned when I got in. She put her book down and checked the time.

"Finish early today?" she asked.

"Yeah," I said, hoping she wouldn't ask me any questions.

"Oh." She started the van up. "Figured he would want to maximize every session."

"I don't want to do the group sessions anymore."

"What?"

"They aren't helping me. They're making me worse."

"Sara—"

"I can't be around other kids like me," I said sharply. "I don't want to be like them."

She sighed. "Okay. We'll talk more tomorrow. But I won't force you to do anything."

I had three new rules when I got home:

139. Stay away from other crazy kids.

140. Especially Erin.

141. Never accept that you are different.

I stared at the last one. I had variations on it throughout the list. But this one was about as clear as it could get. It was the opposite of what Erin had told me. She was okay with being different, or at least she was trying to make it seem like that. But it wasn't helping either of us.

Getting better was the goal. The only goal: Make the Games go away.

I had my rules out for another reason. I crossed off Rule #1.

1. ~~Stop taking the pills.~~

I fished in my pocket and pulled out my two nighttime pills, partially dissolved like little misshapen teeth. I had stuck them under my tongue and spit them out when my mom wasn't looking. It was time to follow my rules. Time to be normal. I put the pills in my drawer and lay down in bed, smiling. Tomorrow I would be normal. Finally.

But I found it hard to sleep. I lay there in the dark and tossed and turned and finally got up and went downstairs. My father was sleeping on the couch, empty bottles scattered around him. I sat down by his legs and just stared at the TV, not really seeing anything but the blue on the walls around me. He stirred.

"Sara?" he mumbled. "What are you doing?"

"Can't sleep."

He yawned and sat up, rubbing his eyes. "Everything all right?"

"Yeah. Just . . . can't sleep."

He nodded and ran two calloused hands down his face, pulling his lips down and letting out a tired, protracted groan. Stubble was turning to patchy beard, and his eyes looked heavy.

"We got to try," he said. "School for you tomorrow. Work for me. Come on now."

"Was I always like this?"

He looked at me, frowning. "What?"

"Was I always like this? Even when I was a baby? Was I born sick?"

He stared at me for a moment, then slid closer and put his arm around me.

"You cried a lot, I guess," he said. "But we never had any other kids . . . maybe they all cry that much. I don't know. You were temperamental. Still are, I think, but you come by that honestly enough. Most things, actually. What are you asking me, Sara?"

I kept my eyes on the TV. "I want to know if I have a chance."

"A chance for what?"

"To get better. I'm trying. Sometimes I feel like I am, but then it goes away again."

He frowned. "Is this about the other night? With your friend?"

"It's about every night."

"I don't know how to make the anxiety stop, Sara. I wish I did. I leave that to Dr. Ring. But I know that I love you as you are. All of that stuff sucks. I know. But it doesn't change who you are. Smart and funny and kind. Nothing changes any of that."

I pulled away from him. "Of course it does—"

"How do you know?" he asked. "You've been dealing with it your whole life." He took my shoulder and smiled. "I told you, you're strong. You'll be just fine."

"I want to be better."

He laughed. "Better than what? If that is your goal, it never stops. When is enough?"

I thought about that. I just wanted to be better than I was now, of course, to be like the other kids at school. But what did that mean? How would I know when I got there? How would I know what they thought or felt?

I had to aim for something. Happiness, maybe. I wasn't happy as Psycho Sara.

That I knew, at least.

He patted my leg. "Now, off to bed. Or I will have to tickle you until you flee."

"But—"

He tickled my side until I squealed, and then he scooped me up in his arms and started upstairs, the floors creaking beneath us. He lay me back in bed and kissed me on the forehead.

"Good night, Sara."

"Good night." I turned to him as he walked out. "Dad?"

"Yeah?"

"You should shower before work tomorrow. You smell like an old dishcloth."

He burst into laughter. "Well, at least you're honest. If nothing else, hold on to that."

He smelled his armpit, pretended to faint, and made his way back downstairs.

"I will be happy," I said to the room. "When I am better. Tomorrow I'll be better."

CHAPTER 21

NOT EVERYONE LIKES VISITORS

I didn't take my morning pills, either. I tucked them under my tongue, went upstairs, and added them to my little pile. I felt heavy already, and as if there were little sparks under my skin, but I decided I was imagining that. I had been taking pills for six years. It would be hard to just stop.

I sat in my room and stared at my rules and said again and again, "You are better."

I went to school on Friday, and the heaviness deepened, and I had a panic attack, but I decided that was to be expected. When I got home, I skipped my nighttime pill too, and I had another panic attack before bed. But when it ended, I just stared up at the ceiling and said "You are better" through the tears. I fell asleep when the sun came up and woke late in the morning.

It was Saturday, so I went to the park at one. I stood

there for about an hour, shivering, but there was no sign of James. Just me and a slide and a November wind. I felt a little strange, but I decided it was nothing. I was on my way home when I remembered that he had come to my house uninvited. He had just looked up my address and showed up. And he was normal.

I knew his address. I could stop by.

I chewed my nails for a minute or two and then made a decision.

I started for his street. We'd gotten another snowfall and then some rain, and now it was halfway-snow: brown and wet and receding into gutters. I splashed along the sidewalk and shoved my hands deep into my pockets, trying to come up with an excuse to visit. I was in the neighborhood? I had new jeans? What was happening to me? Okay . . . I wanted to see how you were doing? Yeah, that might just work.

I got to James's street in about fifteen minutes. The houses were smaller there and connected. His was a duplex with pink bricks and a gravel driveway. There was a sign on the front door that said WELCOME, which I thought was encouraging.

I took a deep breath and went to the door. I hoped James would answer. Anyone else would be tricky. I rang the doorbell and waited, feeling my stomach tie itself into a knot.

A woman opened the door. "Hello, sweetie," she said. "What can I do for you?"

I really hadn't planned this out well. She seemed nice,

but she was new and big and her eyes were like James's except sharper. I felt like I was shrinking beneath her.

I was hoping James had described me as his mute friend, so I made some quick hand gestures Ms. Hugger had taught me for day-to-day use. It was sort of the sign for "Is your son here?" but she obviously didn't know sign language. She looked both ways down the street.

"Are you . . . can you speak?" she asked.

I shook my head. I was starting to sweat. Could I leave?

"Hmm," she said. "No problem. I'll call Lily. You're a bit older than most of her friends, but—"

I shook my head again, and this time she frowned.

"For James?"

I nodded.

"Oh," she said uncertainly. "He didn't say you were coming. He's in the back with some friends from school. Well, you must be from his school too. That boy does seem to be popular."

I just nodded. I guess he didn't mention his mute friend after all.

She smiled. "Head round back, dear."

I started onto the gravel driveway. As I rounded the side of the house, I heard voices and laughter. I thought about leaving again. Even if I didn't talk, maybe his friends wouldn't care. Maybe I *could* talk. Why not? I was making so much progress.

I tried to steady myself, then stepped into the backyard, putting on a smile.

James and three others were standing in a circle, throwing the football. There was another boy and two girls. James was laughing and about to throw to one of the girls when he saw me.

His eyes widened and he lowered the ball. "Sara?"

The other three turned to me. The girls looked at each other as James hurried over.

"What are you doing here?" he whispered.

"I came to say hi," I said, looking down so they wouldn't see me talking.

I wasn't sure why he looked so upset.

"Who is that?" one of the girls asked.

"A neighbor," James replied curtly, which wasn't very specific or accurate.

He took my arm and led me back toward the driveway. His fingers were squeezing hard enough to hurt. He didn't even look at me as the yard slipped out of view. He stopped there.

"How do you know where I live?" he whispered.

I glanced behind him to make sure we were alone. "I looked it up."

He ran a hand over his face and looked at the closest window.

"You can't just come here. Now Mom's going to be asking

and Jones has seen you, and the girls. Those girls aren't nice, Sara. They talk. And Jones is going to ask around . . . ugh. Man."

"You came to my house," I said. I didn't know if that was for him or me.

Obviously, I was wrong to come here. How could I have known that when he had come to my house? I didn't have a rule for that yet.

"It's different. I'm not trying to be mean here. It's just . . . I got my own things."

I had my own things too, but I never held it against him.

"Okay," I said. "Well, I just wanted to say hi and see how you were doing . . ."

"Promise me you won't come back here."

That stung because I knew from TV that friends invited each other over. Crushes, too. I felt my stomach twisting up and a ball in my throat, but I tried not to show it. I just stared at him.

"Ever?" I asked.

He fidgeted. "Unless I tell you it's okay. But better to not come here. We go to the park."

"I thought . . . I thought you wanted to hang out more. I could meet your friends—"

James stared at me like I was crazy. I felt sick. I knew that look. Took you long enough, James.

"We'll hang out next Saturday," James said. "Or maybe earlier. I'll come by."

"Okay," I said.

My voice was cracking, but I got the word out.

He shifted and looked back at the yard. "So, I'll stop in and—"

"I have to get going," I said, starting down the driveway. "See you later."

"Sorry," he called after me, "it's just a bad time. I'll see you."

And then he went back to the yard. Tears came down, and I wondered if they would become brown and wet in the gutters too. I was confused. James had said I wasn't crazy, and that I was smart, and that he was my friend. I had wanted to believe him. But you don't hide your friends. At least that's what I thought. But I've only ever had one other one, so how would I know?

As I cried, I remembered something Sara used to know: Talking gets you hurt.

That night I stared at myself in the mirror and I hated everything I saw. And I cried and played every Game one after another until I was lying on the floor sweating. When my mom called me for my pills, I took them right away and forced a smile and then went back to my room and cried again. One of them was a calming pill, and in an hour or so, I lay still and tired.

"You will never be normal, Psycho Sara," I whispered to the darkness.

I didn't do much on Sunday. My mom asked me what was wrong, but I didn't tell her.

I sat on the couch with my dad. I watched the glass bottle garden grow. I watched football, but not really. I just sat there and thought that maybe *I* had been pretending, not Erin.

That night, I sat by my phone and stared at the screen. Then I texted her.

I'm sorry, Star Child. Can I still be one?

She didn't text me back. I lay down, staring at the ceiling. I had never felt more alone.

My phone buzzed by my head, and I stared at it, almost afraid to read. Afraid that she would tell me to leave her alone for good. It must have been a few minutes. Then I opened it.

Tenet #1. You are a Star Child for life.

I smiled, and the screen blurred. I promised myself I wouldn't forget that again.

CHAPTER 22

GOOD-BYE

She came over Monday night. As soon as I opened the door, she hugged me and dragged me upstairs and made me tell her everything that had happened since our fight. When I got to James, she stormed around the room, ranting that boys are jerks.

When she finally stopped, she turned back to me and stopped. "Are you crying?"

"No," I said quickly, wiping my nose. "Maybe. I just . . . it's nice to have a friend again."

She took me by the shoulders. "Sara something Malvern. What's your middle name?"

"Lynn."

"Sara Lynn Malvern. Do you think I would choose just anyone to be my bestie? Yes, at first your mutism was a real bonus. I could just talk and you couldn't talk back and tell me I look weird like everyone else does. But then I got to know you, and you know what . . . you are brilliant. And funny. And crazy, yes. But so am I. Who cares? We are Star Children, Sara. We don't need to be ashamed of it."

"I know, but—"

She shook me, holding my gaze. "I want you to say Sara Malvern is awesome. Out loud."

I laughed. "What?"

"Say it. Sara Malvern is awesome."

"I don't think—"

"Say it!" she demanded.

"Sara Malvern is awesome," I said quietly.

"Louder."

"Sara Malvern is awe—"

"Louder!"

"Sara Malvern is awesome!" I shouted as loud as I could, and burst out laughing.

"That's better," she said approvingly. "And don't you forget it, either. No matter what."

"I'll try."

"Do or do not. There is no try."

"Thank you, Yoda."

"You're welcome." She straightened up. "Now, we need ice cream. Do you have any?"

"I think so—"

"Excellent. We will eat all of it and watch a Ryan Gosling movie."

I groaned. "We've seen them all—"

"You need eye candy," she cut in. "Trust me, I've suffered heartbreak before."

"You have?"

She grabbed my arm and pulled me toward the door. "No. But I've watched *The Notebook* so many times I basically lived it. What?"

I was staring at her arm. The sleeve was rolled up, and there was bruising all along the skin. It was purple and green and black, and it looked painful. It looked like someone had grabbed her.

I had a feeling I knew who that someone was.

She rolled her sleeve down and forced a smile. "Wrestling practice."

"You wrestle?"

"I'm giving it a try. At school. Have been for a while. We don't do meets or anything."

I watched her head for the door. That had sounded strangely . . . rehearsed. Like she had told that story before. It also sounded like a lie. I knew I should leave it. She had asked me to.

But maybe I could help her. I had promised that I would.

"Erin . . . did your dad do that to you?"

She stopped at the doorway, keeping her back to me. She let the silence hold.

"Why do you say that?" she asked finally.

"I saw him at the birthday . . . and . . . I don't know. Just asking. You can tell me, Erin."

She sighed and turned back. "He gets mad sometimes. That's all."

"The bruise on your hip . . ."

"Yeah," she said quietly. "It's not a big deal. Best friend secret. Okay?"

"But—"

"Please?"

The way she said it made me flinch. But she didn't make me promise.

"Okay."

I followed her downstairs. We ate ice cream and watched two movies, and I said nothing about the bruises, but my eyes kept going to her arm. Those were just the bruises I could see.

How many more were there?

James came over unannounced on Tuesday afternoon. My mom answered the door, and he asked if I would go for a walk. I said yes because I didn't want my mom to overhear us. I put on a scarf and a jacket, and we walked down the street in silence. His mouth kept opening but saying nothing, and his hands moved around awkwardly, from pocket to head to pocket again.

Finally, when we rounded the corner, he stopped and turned to me and met my eyes.

"Sara, I'm sorry about the other day."

I stopped too. "It's fine."

"I shouldn't have acted like that. I know. I feel bad."

I looked at him. No plaid. No bags under the eyes. No sadness. That James was gone. He was feeling better, and he didn't need a crazy girl to help talk him through.

"I should get back," I said.

"Sara . . . aren't we going to talk? How have you been doing—"

I turned away. I could feel him looking at me.

"I feel terrible," he said. "I meant what I said all those times. I did."

"Not all of it."

"Sara—"

"I don't have a lot of people in my life," I said, staring at the road, but not walking, not yet. "But I don't need halves. I can't be friends with James in the park but not James at home."

James tried to take my hand, but I stepped away. There were tears in his eyes now.

"I just need time to explain things to people. You helped me, and I owe you. . . ."

"I'm glad I helped you," I said. "You don't owe me anything. It was a nice time away."

"Away from what?" he asked, wiping his nose.

"From Sara Malvern."

Then I started back down the road for home.

"Good-bye, James."

As I walked away, he got smaller and smaller behind me until he was nothing at all.

NOTE
(ON FRIENDSHIP)

You might be thinking, *Sara, you only have two friends. Can't you give him another chance?*

But when you spend most of your life being silent to protect yourself and then the first boy to come along makes your heart hurt, then you could probably be forgiven for being rash.

Maybe it was a mistake to give up on him so easily. I don't know.

But Erin told me I was special, and I guess I wanted *all* my friends to think that.

CHAPTER 23

PLANS

I went back to group therapy on Thursday, and Dr. Ring smiled when I sat down next to Erin.

"Now," he said, opening his notebook and readying his pen. "I have a few things I want to touch on, but let's just check in with everyone first. Erin, did you have a productive week?"

She glanced at me and smiled. "I think so."

"It's good to work through issues," Dr. Ring agreed. "Especially with friends."

Erin leaned into my shoulder. "It's so good to have the dynamic duo together again," she said softly. "It's been a roller coaster."

"It was really only a week."

"I know," she replied. "It was agonizing."

I bit back a laugh.

"I thought we might talk about family this week," Dr. Ring said. "How we can help them understand our issues. Strategies for helping them help you. We all need a good support system."

I couldn't help it. I glanced at Erin's arms, which were covered with a long-sleeve shirt. She must have noticed, because she tucked her hands in her lap, keeping her eyes firmly on Dr. Ring. I had been thinking about the bruises since Monday. And about my promise to help her.

On the way to the parking lot Erin linked her arm with mine.

"Chill this weekend?" she said. "We could go to the movies."

I opened my mouth to argue, and she just waved me away and laughed.

"Kidding. We are clearly going to ostracize ourselves from society for a while. Your house."

"Good," I said. I hesitated. "Erin?"

"Yeah?"

"Have you ever told anyone . . . about your dad?"

She glanced behind me as we headed for the curb. My mom was parked nearby, reading, and her dad was waiting in his car in front of the office. I could see his face in the orange glare.

"No," she said curtly, turning to face me. "I don't need to."

"Your mom—"

"No. Well, some. It's nothing. He gets mad sometimes, like I said. At everyone, but me the most. He gets frustrated about my . . . stuff. The picking. He is trying to help. It's fine. Really."

She was talking even faster than usual.

I frowned. "But—"

"Sara, just leave it, okay. I love you, bestie, but I don't need your help with this. Please."

"Okay," I said, flushing. "Sorry."

She hugged me and started for the car. "See you Saturday. Buy more ice cream."

They drove off. I watched them until they were out of sight. I should have left it alone.

But I had the tenets to think of, along with the promise.

And those tenets said that I needed to help.

"Daddy?"

He was making coffee and yawning. It was almost dinnertime, but he had fallen asleep on the couch after work and slept for two hours. Mom was going to be out late with her friends.

"Yeah?"

I hesitated. I had decided to help Erin, but I didn't want to just go and tell an adult about everything. For one thing, they might not believe me. Erin was clearly not going to say anything, and her mom either knew or believed the stories about wrestling. So how could I prove her dad was hurting her if Erin would just lie about it? I had done some research on my mom's laptop when I got home. My parents *could* call Child Protective Services. They might launch an investigation and find something. But then it got tricky. Maybe they would take Erin away from him, but they might take her away from her mom, too. And then what?

No matter what, Erin would know I was responsible. And she would hate me forever if she got put in a foster home. There was no way to tell an adult without getting it reported.

This was the right choice. The safe one. But . . . I wondered if there was a way I could make it easier on Erin. If I could let *her* make the choice. My efforts to convince her to tell weren't working. But if I got evidence to *prove* he was hurting her, that might be different. I could show it to Erin and give her the chance to report it or tell her mom. That way maybe Erin could stay at home with her family, and she wouldn't get hit anymore, and she might not hate me.

Well, not as much, anyway. So, it was time to start.

"Can I get a GoPro?" I asked.

He yawned again and took a deep sip of coffee. "A what?"

"It's a camera. It has a really long battery so you can film for a long time."

"Why would you want that?"

This wasn't a lie, I reminded myself. I was just bending the truth.

"Erin and I are working on something. A movie. I'm the director. She's the star." I forced a smile. "They're not that expensive. Early Christmas gift? Oh, and maybe a recorder. Or two."

"A recorder—"

"Sound is important. It's a . . . documentary. On family life for the mentally ill."

Oh, that was low. I was supposed to save that as a last resort. But it worked.

He took another drink of coffee, watching me. "Is it on . . . our family?"

"Hers."

He motioned me to the table and sat down heavily. "I don't like when you say *ill*."

"Right. Mentally . . . unhealthy?"

"Mentally unique," he said, though he grinned. "You're a bugger. All right. What store?"

"Just need your credit card. I can order it all online."

He sighed. "Naturally. Go get it out of my wallet. Try not to put me on the streets."

"Love you, Daddy," I said, starting for the front closet.

He caught my arm. "Sara, your mom and I are fine."

"You said that already."

"And I say it again," he muttered, meeting my eyes. "But

even if that changed, it wouldn't affect how we feel about you. You are the priority. But things can . . . do . . . change."

I thought about that. There was something in his voice that worried me. Defeat, maybe.

"You wouldn't leave without me, right?" I asked him quietly.

"Never," he said.

"Promise?"

"I promise," he said.

I gave him a hug. "If you need to leave, I'll come with you. Anywhere."

"I know," he said into my shoulder. "Now go get your film equipment, Spielberg."

I didn't feel good about bending the truth. But as I ordered the camera and recording devices, I was already planning. Get to Erin's, plant the equipment, and gather my evidence.

And a small part of me knew that maybe *two* families were on their way to breaking.

As I sat with Erin on Saturday night, eating ice cream and watching *Drive*, I tried to think of a plan.

"You know," Erin said, mouth full of ice cream, "I might be a criminal if I could date Ryan Gosling. Not like, murder or anything, but maybe a robber. Like, I would think about it."

I just nodded, only half listening.

"I told Penny off today. You know that evil eighth grader I told you about? She put her fingers over her eyebrows and pretended to be me."

I glanced at her. "What did you do?"

"I told her she was a soulless wench. I really said wench. I've been playing Warcraft."

I laughed without thinking, covering my mouth. "What did she say?"

"Not much. I think she was trying to figure out what a wench was." She sighed dramatically. "It's tough being brilliant. Well, you know. I saw your test scores on your desk."

"You did?"

Ms. Hugger did give me a lot of tests. And I didn't get much wrong. Ever.

"Yeah. Even your state ones. You're like a prodigy. Why didn't you tell me?"

"I don't know—"

"Because you have no confidence, silly! Rhetorical question. Are you doing your drill?"

She had asked me to tell my reflection I was awesome every night before bed.

"Yes—"

"Keep doing it. Beautiful, smart, bizarrely funny. You should be full of yourself."

I laughed. "You forgot crazy."

"So? Derek Hogan gets to be cocky, and he has the personality of that popcorn bowl." She reached out and plunked some in her mouth. "Listen, I don't always have the confidence either. I told you I cry in the stupid mirror sometimes. I feel ugly and I pick and then I feel uglier. The point is this: I have issues. But that's *my* thing. I'm working on it. Nobody else gets to tell me what I am."

I stared at her. I thought of all the names. Retard. Freak. Psycho Sara. People had been telling me what I was my whole life. And I had believed those names—*seen* myself as them. I had hated myself and made all my rules trying to become someone other than Psycho Sara. My own inner voice referred to me like that.

But maybe I could change that voice.

She looked at me, smiling. "You look spacey, Star Child."

"I am," I murmured. "I am a Star Child."

She shook my wrist, sending the bracelet jangling. "Obvi."

To her, I had been one for weeks. But not to me. Not fully. Not until that moment, watching the little stars dangle from my wrist. A Star Child was special. A Star Child didn't have to be normal. They *couldn't* be. Which meant there was something I had to do. Right now.

"Come with me," I said, heading to my room.

Erin jumped up after me. "What are you doing? Why do you look kind of murderous?"

"Because I need to destroy something."

She followed me up the stairs. "Sweet."

I led her into my room, opened my drawer, and took out the notebook. *The Rules for Being Normal.* The guidelines I had tried to use for the last two years. Tried and always failed.

I opened the first page and showed it to her. She read them silently, shaking her head.

"How many?" she asked quietly.

"One hundred and fifty-four."

Erin grinned. "Time to die, normal rules."

I ripped the page out and tore it up. Then the next. They all came out; then I tore those up too. Soon we were both laughing and ripping and sending pieces everywhere until the carpet looked like snow. I looked around, giggling.

Erin had a scrap in her hair. She was grinning wildly.

"How will you live now?" she asked.

"By the Tenets of Star Children," I replied. "Oh, that reminds me."

I took out the tenets and grabbed a pen. Then I added one more to make it five.

A Star Child never gives up, even when it is really, really, hard.

Erin read it and smiled. "Perfect. They're done."

"We are bound by the five grand tenets," I said, saluting. "I am a Star Child until death."

She saluted back. "Welcome aboard. Question number one: Do you have a vacuum?"

I looked around at the mess, and I started laughing again until my eyes watered.

She joined in, and we stood there in the paper snow, laughing like crazy.

CHAPTER 24

A NATURAL SPY

My package arrived on Tuesday. As soon as my dad handed it to me, I ran to my room to test it. The confetti was gone, and the rules with them. The tenets were the only guidelines I had left.

I ripped open the package and examined its contents, satisfied. It was the smallest GoPro available, and the recording devices were even smaller, about the size of a USB stick. Those would be easy to hide, but the camera was going to be tricky. I needed clear sightlines, obviously, and I would have to choose a spot wisely—somewhere the camera could see but not be seen.

I experimented with them until I was comfortable, and then I made my plans.

One bonus was that I was so busy planning my mission that I didn't have time to play many Games during the week.

Ms. Hugger and I even ate lunch in the cafeteria.

There was a small change. Nothing big. Nothing visible. Just because I was an official Star Child didn't mean I was going to start talking to people or tap dancing in the hallways. But it did mean that I didn't spend half the day wishing I was anywhere but the Crazy Box. It meant I wasn't watching to see who was whispering "Psycho Sara" or calling me a freak when I walked by.

And that small change made a big difference in my day. I wasn't looking for anyone to tell me what I was. That was my job, and I had decided to listen to Erin: Sara was awesome.

When I had the new devices organized, I picked up my cell phone. Now for Part B.

Sara: Want to hang out this week?

Erin: Obvi!! When?

Sara: Tomorrow night?

Erin: Wednesday hangouts. Love it. Take that, school night. What time should I come?

This was where I had to bend the truth again. *It's for the greater good,* I reminded myself. Always telling the truth wasn't technically a tenet. But helping a fellow Star Child was.

Sara: My parents are going out. I was wondering if I could come there for a bit?

Erin: Oh. Sure. You remember that my house is messy and my family sucks, right?

Sara: Yeah.

Erin: Okay. Are they going to drop you off? When?

Sara: After dinner. 7?

Erin: It's a date. If you bring ice cream, it will not be turned away.

Sara: Noted.

I put the phone down and sighed. I didn't like lying to Erin, but that was about to be the least of our issues. Could I get away with my spying? Could I get my evidence back again? And even if I did, how would she react? Probably by punching me in the nose. I chewed on my nails.

It wasn't too late. I could return the spying equipment. I could keep Erin's secret.

I went to the bathroom. It was almost nine, so I brushed my teeth for bed and stared in the mirror, thinking. This was going to end badly. One way or the other, I was going to hurt Erin. But her father was hurting her worse. I thought of the mottled bruises. The birthday party.

That look on his face while he held her. It made my skin crawl.

How could I be a Star Child if I let him hurt my friend? How could I like myself if I kept something like that a secret? I couldn't. I wouldn't. I spit out my toothpaste and stared at myself.

"You are awesome, Sara Malvern," I said.

I didn't sleep well. I rolled around for hours and had a panic attack and felt spacey after that. My limbs felt heavy.

But I kept saying it anyway. This was all a test. Part of the process.

A Star Child had to be strong.

"You are awesome," I whispered, sleep finally pulling at my eyes. "You are strong."

"Can I use your bathroom?" I said.

We were sitting on the carpet in Erin's room, doodling and talking and debating whether we needed any more tenets. Erin looked tired today. She had pulled more hair in the last few days. Her eyebrows were basically gone again now, aside from some stubble, and her lashes, too. I didn't say anything. She was working on that. She was getting help.

Dr. Ring knew about *that*.

But for the third time, I had spotted a bruise. It was at the base of her neck, probably extending out from her shoulder. She had seen me looking and put her hoodie back on, forcing a smile. Too late. If I hadn't been sure of going ahead with the plan before, I was now.

"No," she said dryly, "you have to go pee in the corner."

"Manners."

"Manners are for regular people. We have higher things on the mind."

I snorted and headed for the door. "Be right back. Going to check my cell phone too . . . I left it in my jacket downstairs. I just want to make sure my parents didn't send me any updates."

"What do you want . . . a hall pass?" she said, drawing a star on her homework.

"If you have one—"

"Go," she said, laughing and waving me away. "I will add a new tenet in your absence. No need to announce bathroom breaks. Also, one must always bring the ice cream when—"

I left her talking to herself and headed downstairs. My jacket was in the closet, and the camera and one of the audio recorders were stuffed in my pockets. The other recorder was now sitting safely under Erin's bed, slipped there while she was drawing. It had twenty-four hours of battery life, so her bedroom was covered for a full day. That had been the easy part.

Now I had to expand my range.

I shoved the audio recorder in my jeans pocket and scanned the main floor, GoPro in hand. It was small, black, and square, like a pencil sharpener. It was the most inconspicuous one I could find. But this was trickier than I thought. The battery life had been the first problem—only four hours even on the lowest resolution—but I took my father's external battery charger. He bought it for his cell phone while he was at work, but I convinced him my documentary was more important. With that plugged in as well, I could get a full twelve hours. It wasn't much, but it would have to do. But that meant hiding the camera and the charger.

Taking a last look around, I chose my spot.

The living room—I guessed that's what it was, since there was no furniture—was to the right side of the foyer, and there was a pile of still-taped boxes that looked like they had been thrown there on moving day and never touched again. There was even a layer of dust on them.

I tucked the camera in the middle of them, mostly shadowed, and made sure it was pointed to capture the widest possible angle. It now covered the living room, the foyer, the staircase, and the additional room on the other side of the foyer, which had a dining table.

My heart was pounding as I hurried back to the stairs again. I could hear a TV on somewhere down the hall—there was another room next to the kitchen where they had a den. Her parents were probably there. I fished into my pocket, debating where to put the other audio recorder. Maybe the kitchen?

How could I get there unseen?

The basement door suddenly flew open, and her brother emerged, frowning at me.

"Jeez, you scared me," he muttered. "Sara, right? The . . . uh . . . shy girl?"

I nodded.

He looked at me for a moment, as if realizing I was alone. "You need something?"

I shook my head. I could feel my body seizing up. No. Now was not the time for Games.

You are a Star Child. You have a mission. Just get back to the stairs.

I turned and hurried upstairs again, hearing a distinct snort behind me. The other recorder would just have to go upstairs too. I went to the bathroom and closed the door, trying to breathe. My hands on the counter, I looked at myself in the mirror. *You are awesome. You are awesome.*

I felt like I was going to pee myself. But after a quick splash of water, I managed to keep the Game at bay. Danger Game, maybe. That would not have been a good thing.

I tucked the last recorder under the sink, way at the back behind the towels and baskets of toiletries, and then went back to Erin's bedroom. She glanced up, looking out into the hallway.

"Did I hear my cursed brother?"

"He just asked if I needed anything."

"Naturally. Like a knife in the back." She yawned. "We need another TV. Your house this weekend. Mine is awful."

I sat down on the bed, trying to think. "Sure. Well, if my parents aren't out."

"Again?" she muttered. "Party animals. Yeah, well, we can play it by ear."

"Erin!" her mother shouted up the stairs. "It's a school night!"

She sighed dramatically. "Do you see what I must live with? Your parents back yet?"

"Yeah. I'll text them for a ride."

Ten minutes later, we were waiting by the door. I tried not to look at the GoPro. I was already regretting the spot. It seemed so obvious now. Why couldn't I just use the stupid audio recorders? They would have been enough. I had gotten greedy and now I was going to get caught.

The TV was still playing in the background.

Then I heard her dad. "—thinks she can spy on me? Thinks she's clever. I know where she lives—"

My breathing picked up. It was the Danger Game. That was all.

I tried to focus on Erin.

"She's not going to leave this house," her father was saying now.

No, he wasn't. He was just watching TV.

I put my hands on the door, trying to smile at Erin. "You find it hot in here?"

She frowned. "No. You do look a bit flushed."

"Hold her at the door," her father was saying.

Maybe. It was so hard to tell. Did he say that, or did I imagine it? Was he coming for me?

The Danger Game won out. I hurried outside, pulling my jacket tight. It was cold out. Freezing. But I walked to the driveway anyway, trying not to run away or scream.

"You all right, bestie?" Erin asked, propping the door open.

"Fine. Just hot. Sara break."

"Right," she said dryly. "Well, your timing was good."

I turned and saw my dad pulling into the driveway. My brain was still telling me to run, but I just smiled again, waved, and climbed into the car, breathing only when the door was locked.

"Fun night?" my dad asked, giving Erin a wave.

"Yeah," I murmured. "It was great."

NOTE
(ON MY SKILLS
AS A DETECTIVE)

You might be thinking: Crazy girl, what do you know about detective work? And yes, hiding a camera and recording devices around a friend's house in an attempt to spy on her family does sound crazy. Actually, it probably is. I don't recommend that plan. Like, ever. But it was too late now. And thinking about it, I really should have hidden the camera anywhere but a pile of boxes that technically *have* to be moved at some time in the future to unpack them. Fiddlesticks.

Anyway, that wasn't the point of this note. The point is that I love detective stories. Of my 619 books, 127 of them are Nancy Drew, Hardy Boys, or good old Mr. Holmes. They were always my favorite, and for a very specific reason: The detectives always solve the problem. There is a mystery, they solve it, and everyone is happy. Even tough ones. They just need a little more time.

Also, Nancy never let a bad guy escape.

I wasn't about to either.

CHAPTER 25

MODEL BEHAVIOR

I chewed my nails through most of the group session on Thursday. Even Peter seemed to notice. Dr. Ring asked me if I was nervous about something four times, and four times I shook my head.

"You're going to have stubs for fingers soon," Erin whispered.

I withdrew my finger and grimaced. "Just . . . thinking."

"About?"

"Umm. Mental health?"

She snorted. "Well, you're in the right place."

Dr. Ring looked up from his notes. The topic today was communication, so I guess it was a good day to chat. He put his pen back down and surveyed the room, stopping on Erin.

"Mental disorders can make us feel alone. As a result, relationships are key to overcoming our issues. It's not how many friends or family members you have. It's the type. One honest relationship is worth a thousand not."

Erin grinned. "Yes, Dr. Ring, we are the bestest of besties. We know."

"I think I just threw up in my mouth," Peter grumbled.

"Better than the floor," Erin said. "*Someone* took a chance on me as a friend."

She distinctly looked at Taisha and Mel, who both flushed and turned away.

"Let's stay on topic," Dr. Ring said quickly, eyeing the group. "The point is to seek out people you can trust. Of all my patients, those who find connections and purpose heal best."

Purpose. I thought about that and glanced at Erin, but she just shook her head. I had asked her yesterday if she ever thought about sharing the Star Child theory with the rest of the group. It had taken a while to sink in, but the theory had made me feel better. I felt like I belonged.

But Erin said the others weren't "ready for the truth." We both knew that the real risk was they would laugh and make fun of us. Well, her. I still wasn't talking to them, so she had to be the messenger. I hadn't added a single person to my talk list since James, and I was fine with that. Like Dr. Ring said . . . I had to be selective. I did think of James still. A lot. I wondered if he would show up again. But I knew he wouldn't.

I guess hope had to be used selectively too. I couldn't use it all up on one boy.

At the end of the session, Erin and I left together. She had shared a lot tonight. . . . Friendship and trust and communicating seemed to be her favorite topics. The irony was not lost on me. I was planning on testing all three. First things first. I needed to tell another lie.

I took out my cell phone and pretended to read a text message. "Uh-oh."

"What?"

I grimaced. "My mom is running late. Can't get me for another hour. Dad is out too."

"No problem. We can drop you off—"

"I don't have a key," I said, frowning. "Maybe I can stick around here—"

"Don't be stupid," she cut in. "Just come to my place and they can grab you from there."

"Is that okay?"

I eyed the car nervously, but it was her mom in the driver's seat tonight.

"Obvi. Come on."

She quickly explained the situation to her mom, who just waved us in. I tried to keep the guilt off my face. It was all simple enough: I told my mom that Erin invited me over for an hour to work on our movie—she knew about my "documentary" now and didn't exactly approve—and asked if she could get me from there. I could have waited until the weekend, but the longer the camera and the recorders were there, the better the chance of being found. I had to move fast.

"I washed your gym clothes tonight," her mom said. "Wrestling tomorrow?"

Erin paused. Just for a second. "Yeah. Over lunch, I think."

"Are we going to get to see a meet one day or—"

"Maybe," she said. "Still not very good."

Her mom glanced in the mirror and shook her head. "Maybe you could try another—"

"No," she said. "I like wrestling. Listen, I was talking about Peter the Grump—"

I listened to her in silence. Her mom really thought she was wrestling. It seemed ridiculous—but maybe she wanted to believe it. But it made my plan all the more important. I needed to show her something she couldn't ignore. Either her, or the police.

I stared out the window, running through my plan. I needed to collect all three devices within the hour. Without being seen. Then I needed to get them home safely and check them for evidence. And if I didn't get anything, then I had to do this all over again. That would be bad.

There had been no Games in group therapy, and I had to try to keep it together for a little while longer. But the closer we got to Erin's house, the more I felt my insides writhing.

Stay focused, I told myself. *You have a mission.*

We pulled into the driveway, and Erin basically pulled me inside and up to her bedroom, closing the door and flopping onto her bed. She sighed and rolled onto her back, glancing at me.

"Group therapy takes it out of me," she said. "It's all the staring, I think."

I sat down on the carpet beside her bed, nodding even as I reached around the back between the frame and the wall. My fingers closed on the audio recorder, and I quickly tucked it into my pocket. One down, two to go. My heart was racing, but I could still pull this off. Maybe.

"You staring at Peter, you mean?" I said.

She coughed and sat up. "I do not stare at Peter!"

"Sometimes you do."

She paused. "He has a sort of a . . . brooding allure."

"Have you been reading *Twilight* again?"

"Yes," she said.

I giggled and climbed up on the bed with her. "I thought you said not to trust boys."

"And I stand by that," she said. "I just like to pretend he's a Cullen."

"He is pale."

"Exactly," she agreed. "And I would not be surprised at all if he was biting people."

I giggled, but there was no more time to waste. I patted my jeans and sighed dramatically.

"Left my phone in my jacket."

"You really stink at that," she said. "Well, I need to get a drink anyway. Come on."

I opened my mouth, but there wasn't much to say to that. I just followed her downstairs, trying to think fast. There was a bathroom off the foyer. That would have to do.

"Got to pee," I said.

"Want a drink?"

"No, thanks," I said, ducking into the bathroom and closing the door.

I waited for a moment, then looked out again. She was in the kitchen around the corner, and the foyer was clear. The GoPro. I had to get that next.

I hurried to the living room and ducked down by the boxes, my breath in my throat. But the camera was still there—right where I left it. I grabbed it just as footsteps rounded the corner.

"Are you peeing on those boxes?" Erin asked.

I looked back, still clutching the GoPro and attached charger. "Umm—"

She walked over, sipping on a juice box. "Don't even know what's in there, really."

"Sorry," I muttered, straightening up and stuffing the GoPro in my pocket. "I just wondered what it was. I was grabbing my phone and saw them. Sorry. I shouldn't just look at—"

"It's fine," she said, laughing. "I totally snooped through your bedroom."

"You did?"

"Uh . . . yeah? How was I supposed to know if you were a serial killer?"

I pursed my lips and then shrugged. "Fair enough."

"Let's go before my parents decide to ask us about our days. Ugh."

We hurried back upstairs, the camera safely tucked away. That was the hard part.

After one more bathroom break upstairs, I had the third recorder safely in hand. Some of the tension seeped away as I came back and sat down at her desk, shifting to keep my now-full pockets out of her view, and reached for my cell phone. I could call for a ride, go home, and inspect my findings. I still needed a bit of luck—I wasn't sure I could bring myself to go through this again. Was twenty-four hours enough time to get evidence? How often was her father getting . . . angry?

The bedroom door swung open. He stepped inside, wearing a thin smile.

My whole body tensed. It felt like the wheel was spinning a hundred miles an hour.

"School night, ladies," he said. "Sara, are your parents home?"

I nodded and got ready to text them. My skin was itching madly. He was staring, smiling.

"I have to go get milk," he said. "I'll drop you off. Save them the trip."

My fingers froze on the screen. I glanced at Erin, who yawned and stood up.

"Come on, Sara—"

"You get ready for bed, missy," he said. "Your mom said you slept in last week."

"I only missed breakfast—"

"Exactly," he replied curtly. "You have to be ready for the day. Come on, Sara."

I could feel the panic taking over. Did he know? Was he going to hurt me, too? I tried to rack my brain for some way out of this, some excuse, but I could never summon words with him staring at me, and even if I could, my brain wasn't working. I just nodded and stood up.

Erin gave me a hug. "Just nod along if he talks," she whispered.

It might have been my imagination, but it sounded like a warning. It occurred to me that Erin hadn't argued with him. She could argue that the sky was orange. But with her father, she gave up right away. I knew why. And that made me angry. Angry enough to push the panic back.

I followed him downstairs to the door.

"You are on Leewood Drive, right?" he asked. "Cindy mentioned."

I nodded, and he smirked as he slipped his shoes on.

"Right . . . silence is golden," he said. "You and I will get along fine."

I waved to Erin and stepped outside, feeling the cold close in on all sides. I tentatively got into the passenger seat, and he started the car, waiting for a minute as the engine warmed up. It was perfectly silent. No talking. No radio. I could feel the GoPro digging into my left thigh. I liked silence, but not today. I just kept my eyes on the garage and tried to remember I was brave.

We pulled out and started down the road. He drove a manual, so I was aware that his strong right arm was constantly moving not far from me. I tried not to flinch. The full weight of what I had done suddenly seemed unbearable. I had spied on a man. A man I knew was dangerous. Me. Sara Malvern. A girl who couldn't go to school without having a panic attack.

What had I been thinking?

I tried to keep it together. The wheel was still spinning, but even though my throat was dry and my chest was tight, it didn't stop. I was in control, for now, and we were heading home.

I was close.

"Erin told me a bit about your condition," he said suddenly. "Conditions, I guess."

I said nothing. My eyes were on the road. *Please, just let me get home.*

"And you know all about hers, of course. Tough to see. Only started the last few years. I often wonder why. A lack of control, I guess. Discipline." He glanced at me. "But who knows?"

I tried to force a smile. My nails were digging into my leg.

"I'm old-fashioned," he continued. "Not into the whole shrink thing. Talking it out. Sometimes I think if she just focused a little more, she could beat it. You know what I mean?"

Clearly, he had never read a thing about mental health. But this wasn't the time for a lesson, even if I could talk to him. I just wanted to go home. We were close now. A block or two.

"What do you guys talk about in your group therapy? Sorry, you can just nod. Does she talk much? About home and school and stuff like that?"

His voice was lower now. I risked a brief glance and saw he was looking at me.

I shook my head.

He smiled. "I find that hard to believe, knowing Erin. Well, she must talk to you a lot." He shifted gears as we turned onto another street. "Does she talk about how it all got started?"

I shook my head again. *Please let me get home.*

"Tough to get a nod out of you," he said dryly. "I was just curious. One day she just seemed to be pulling out hair. Found a clump in the shower. Then the lashes. Horrible stuff."

He pulled onto my street.

"I'm sure you all have stories at the group sessions," he said. "Issues at school. At home. Maybe parents are behind a lot of it. I'll have to try to talk to her again. She can be stubborn."

I pointed at my house, trying to keep my hand from shaking, and he pulled in.

"There we are. I'll wait until you get inside."

He turned to face me fully. His face was half in shadow.

"I hope you and Erin are good for each other," he said. "Maybe you can help each other."

I nodded. There you go, Mr. Stewart. I could nod for that.

I opened the door and swung a leg out.

"We'll have to be honest about the friendship if not," he continued. "We also need positive examples. Behavior to model ourselves after. I'm sure your parents would agree. We'll have to be honest."

I paused for a moment. I knew what he meant. Normal girls. Normal friends. What I had been trying so hard to be. Of course he wanted normal girls. Ones who didn't ask any questions.

Well, bad luck, Mr. Stewart. You got Sara Malvern.

I gave him a smile, closed the door, and hurried inside, not looking back. Then I went right to the couch, sat next to my dad, and slipped under his arm. The Game didn't come.

"I love you, Daddy," I said, resting my head on his shoulder.

"I love you too, Princess," he replied, his voice a little slurred.

I didn't care. He was here. I was safe. I was lucky.

I waited there for an hour or so, and then I went to my room to see what I'd found.

CHAPTER 26

STAR CHILD

I plugged the USB cable from the GoPro to my laptop and sat back, chewing on my nail as the video uploaded. It was long, and a minute or two crawled by, staring at nothing but the loading bar in the darkness.

The recorders were playing beside me. They had little speakers, but they were quiet, so I had both going at once. It probably wasn't proper sleuthing, but I couldn't wait a moment longer. I needed to know if I'd recorded something.

The bathroom recorder was muffled. I had put it too far back in the cabinet. Water ran loudly, and that was about it. The one from Erin's room was better, but I heard only footsteps so far. Shuffling around the bedroom. Beds creaking. Then a familiar voice.

"Not tonight," Erin was saying. "One day at a time. Reassert control. Stay mindful."

I could feel my stomach twisting. She was quoting Dr. Ring, obviously trying not to pull. It felt deeply personal, and I almost wanted to turn it off. Then the video started playing too.

Now my eyes were locked on the screen, the recorders playing on either side.

I stared, absorbed.

I had gotten ten hours and forty-seven minutes. Most were at night when everyone was asleep. I sped up the footage to one and a half speed. A few people walked by. Her brother. Her mother going to bed.

Him.

The sounds didn't match, of course. They were running on different timelines. I watched as the foyer lights blinked out. Just darkness. I sped up the footage to two times. Then three. The hours counted along through the night. It was well past midnight right now too. I kept watching.

"Good night, Erin," Erin's mother said in the bedroom recorder.

Those were running at normal speed—everything was eerily out of order.

"Good night," Erin said.

Water running again. Muffled voices. Was that Erin in the bathroom? I leaned closer.

"—not supposed to do that. Stay mindful. What is wrong with me?"

The last part sounded like a prayer. I had said it so many times.

"I'm sorry, bestie," I whispered. "I'm sorry for spying. But I promised to help you."

The camera was recording darkness. I fast-forwarded to four times. Shuffling from the bedroom recorder again. A bed creaking. My skin was prickling, from anticipation or maybe guilt. The minutes crawled by. Silence and darkness and it seemed all of this was for nothing.

Then a voice.

"How was your night with your friend?"

His voice. I heard the bed groan under new weight. I picked up that recorder and held it close to my ear, the other one forgotten now. The scene began to lighten on the video. Morning was coming there. From the recorder, her father had come to say good night to Erin.

"Good," she said.

"I heard you in the bathroom."

There was silence for a moment.

"I—" she started.

"You did it again."

It wasn't a question. His voice was hard and low. I cringed for her. Morning came.

"I didn't—ow, I didn't—"

Her voice was breaking up. Cracking. Was she crying?

"Don't lie to me," he said. "I told you to let it grow back. I told you to stop—"

"I'm trying—ow, that hurts—"

"It should hurt," he said. His voice was low. "I am trying to help you. This crackpot Dr. Ring obviously isn't. And this girl. You really think hanging out with her is helping? Well?"

"I don't know—"

She was definitely crying now. I could just barely hear the sniffling.

"I don't want to get angry," he said, sounding calm now, even loving. His voice could change so fast. "Did you pull your hair tonight? Answer me honestly, Erin Ashley Stewart."

People started to move around in the video. I slowed it down to two times. Her father came down. Then her mom, then her brother. Erin too. They moved too quickly across the screen.

"I did—" Erin said. She gasped. "I'm sorry."

"Lying doesn't help you get better," he said. "You know I want what is best for you."

"I'm sorry, Daddy—you're hurting my arm—"

His voice got even lower. "I will not have a daughter walking around like a freak because she can't control herself," he said. "Do you understand? I will keep you home. Don't test me."

She gasped again. I could feel my heart breaking for her. *Stop it. Please stop it.*

Erin came onto the screen. So did he. They were standing in the foyer. Normal speed.

"I'll stop," she said. "I will, Daddy. I'm sorry."

In the video, he was facing her in the daylight now. I could see their lips moving. He leaned down, looking at her face. His hand was on her side. They were talking, but I could only hear the recording. Then his hand came up.

It was all so fast. I had to rewind. A balled fist and a hard shot into the side. She looked like she might go down, but he had his hand on her arm, holding her, finger pointed at her face.

My eyes filled with tears.

"Get some sleep," he said in the recording.

The bed creaked. He must have stood up.

"Tomorrow you will get better," he said. There were foot-steps, and muffled crying.

The words hung there. He had said it just like me. Like my prayer.

He left in the video as well, and she stood there alone, wiping her face, and then ran upstairs.

I sat there for a long time. There was nothing else on the video. Not that it mattered. I had gotten what I was look-ing for. She survived *that* daily. I could hardly imagine her strength. I realized I was crying, and I wiped my face with my sleeve. It was soaked. I must have been crying for hours. I hadn't even noticed. The recorders were still playing, but I stopped them, uploaded the files to an unnamed folder on my mom's laptop, and transferred all three onto my phone for a backup.

Then I closed the laptop and lay in bed with my cell phone.

I hadn't showered or brushed my teeth, but I was too tired to care.

Before I fell asleep, I wrote a text message:

Want to come over tomorrow? I need to show you something.

I thought back to the video, and the recordings, and wrote one more message:

Sweet dreams, Star Child.

CHAPTER 27

STARS UPON STARS

I was restless in school the next day. Erin had agreed to come over. I had lain awake for most of the night, thinking about that voice, and even when I did sleep, it was all nightmares. I could feel the fuzziness in my brain today. The bursts of anxiety like firecrackers every few minutes.

I couldn't fold up, though. Not today. I had to help Erin.

And first, I had to completely betray her trust. Even after everything I had seen and heard, I was hesitant. My notebooks were full of stars. I still couldn't decide what to do about it.

How could I lose my one and only friend?

"I've noticed a lot of these lately," Ms. Hugger said.

I looked up and realized she was standing beside my desk. I forced a smile. I had mentioned the Star Child stuff to her, but she wasn't a fan of "pseudoscience," so I'd left it there.

"Just fun to draw," I said.

"You look tired."

"Didn't sleep well," I admitted.

She pulled up a chair and sat down across from me. "Want to talk about it?"

I did. I had already thought about bringing it up with Mom and Dad, but I could never quite figure out how to keep it cryptic. Could I now? I looked at her, halfway through a star.

"Have you ever lost a friend?"

"Yes."

"How?"

"Silly things mostly. Distance for some. Even worse . . . fights or boys for others."

"Did you ever lose one and get them back later?"

"Of course," she said. "What is this about?"

"Would you ever do something bad to keep a friend? Tell a lie? Ignore something?"

"Sara, what is this—"

"Would you?" I asked quietly.

She sighed and leaned back. "I have done that. Lied or ignored. But I shouldn't have."

"Why?"

"Friends are important. You spend a lot of time with them. But you spend way more time with yourself." She smiled. "What is it that Dr. Ring told you about yourself? I liked that one."

"He said the most important relationship in your life is with yourself."

She tapped the desk and got up again, heading to the whiteboard. "So there you go. If keeping a friend means doing something that makes you not like yourself, then it's a bad idea."

She stopped and looked back at me.

"You seem different lately, Sara. I meant to say something last week. I mean, you looked tired today, but still . . . different."

"Different how?"

"More sure of yourself, maybe. You aren't walking around with your head down all day."

"Tired of looking at my shoes, I guess."

She smiled. "That must be it. Well, keep it up. I like seeing you like this."

She went back to her equations on the board, and I watched her, feeling a sudden pressure behind my eyes. She had no idea what that word meant to me, of course. I thought back to my nighttime prayer, the one I said a thousand times: *Tomorrow you will be better.*

I had spent all that time wishing I could magically get better, when I just had to make things better for myself. I had to stop trying to be something I wasn't. I had to stop hating myself and thinking about all the ways I was wrong. I had to stop calling myself Psycho Sara.

My name was Sara Malvern, and I wasn't very normal at all.

I looked down at my notebook, smiling.

Then I finished the star.

She came over at seven. I met her at the door. We hugged and hurried upstairs, and she told me about Kevin, who had most definitely smiled at her today. My laptop was sitting on my desk, and I kept glancing at it, waiting for the right time. But an hour went by, and it never seemed to come. I took three Sara breaks and nearly had a panic attack on the third. I just couldn't face her.

"Having a rough one, huh?" she said when I came back. She was lying on the floor, doodling in a notebook. Stars. Always stars with her. "I had one the other day. It was a doozy."

"What do you do on those days?" I asked hoarsely, trying to control my breathing.

"More hair-pulling. Panic attacks. Or I just get all moody and make my family mad. Of course, in my brother's case that doesn't take much. He called me an idiot yesterday. The irony, Sara."

I smiled and sat down at my desk, fingers tracing across my chest. Another time, I decided. Today wasn't a good day to tell her. She had already asked what I wanted to show her, and I said it wasn't ready yet. It gave me time to think more. I didn't want to lose my friend.

But the computer was behind me. I could remember the voice. The crying.

"You know," Erin said, propping herself up on her elbows. "I was thinking about James."

I frowned. "Why?"

"Oh, I think about how I want to punch him all the time. But this was different. I was thinking how sorry he is going to be. I mean, you're going to grow up to be, like, some beautiful astrophysicist, and he's going to be, like, take me back, and you're going to be, like, too late, loser."

I laughed without thinking. "I don't think that's going to happen."

"Oh, it will. To me, too. Like, we're both Star Kids. Older people respect intelligence."

"The eighth graders call me Psycho Sara too—"

"No, you dipstick. I mean, like, adults. These middle schoolers don't get us." She got up and flung herself onto the bed. "Me, I'm going to be an actress. I decided it. I have the it factor."

"Yes, you do," I agreed.

"And we'll be the dynamic duo. Scientist and celebrity. Beautiful, smart, rich—"

She rolled over to look at the ceiling. Her shirt came up. Just a bit, but enough.

There were bruises on her hip. Yellow and green like nebulous clouds blocking out all the stars. Her shirt was down again in an instant, but I clenched my teeth, mind spinning again.

What if he hurt her again tonight? Tomorrow. The next day. What if he hurt her bad one of these times? Broke something inside or out? What if she lost her starlight and I could have prevented it?

She was still talking. Stories about her career. About how we would be friends at ninety.

I wanted that. And I also wanted to be a Star Child. I wanted to like Sara Malvern.

And I knew it would be hard to like someone who was afraid of telling the truth.

"Erin," I said.

She glanced at me. "What?"

"I want to show you that thing." I tried to swallow, but my throat was dry. "Come here."

She slowly got up. She could probably see the look on my face.

But I had decided. I turned to my computer and opened the edited file. I edited it when I got home—edited so the image and the audio were both at the point that I wanted. They didn't actually line up, but I wanted her to see it just like I had. I wanted her to know that there was no explaining it away.

I took a deep breath that barely seemed to reach my lungs. Then I pressed play.

The video and the voices started at once.

Erin said nothing as they played. She listened and

watched. Her eyes watered. I wanted to hug her or say something, but I didn't. I just sat there and waited, preparing myself.

The encounter in the hallway stopped before the audio recording. Then it was just a black screen, and the voices finally stopping, a bedroom door closing, and a girl crying in the darkness.

Then that was done too, and there was just Erin and me.

"So that's what you were doing," she said. Her voice was so quiet. "I was wondering."

I turned to face her. Her eyes were still on the screen, her hands balled up at her sides.

"I'm sorry," I whispered. "But I told you I was going to help."

"Delete it."

I shook my head. "I already made copies. I won't."

She tightened her fists.

"What are you going to do with it?" she asked. "Did you show it to anybody?"

Her hands were shaking. I waited for the punch.

"Not yet," I said. "I will, but I wanted to show you first. Talk to your mom. You can tell her about the recording if you want. If you don't tell her, or report it, then I'll share it myself."

She stared at me for a moment. "I asked you to leave it alone."

"And you also told me I was a Star Child," I replied. "You asked me to help. So I did."

She ran her hands over her face, and to my surprise, she laughed. It was a sad one, or resigned maybe, but she pulled her hands down across her mouth, eyes still on the screen.

"I don't believe this."

She sounded so betrayed that I stood up, reaching out to her. She stepped away.

"I had to—" I said.

"No, you didn't," she snapped. "You put cameras in our house. You can't just do that. You're going to get in trouble if you report us. That's illegal. It won't even work—"

"Your mom doesn't know, does she?" I asked. "She really thinks you wrestle."

Erin looked at me. I knew before she spoke. "She knows he gets mad."

"And the bruises?"

She flushed. "She doesn't always see them. I'm . . . more careful there, I guess. And when she does . . . I tell her they're from wrestling. She believes me, I think. I thought I could trust you."

"Tell her the truth," I said. "Tell her or I'll send these to Child Protective Services and the police."

She stepped toward me, grabbing my arm. "He's my dad, Sara—"

"And he is hurting my best friend," I said. "So he is going to stop."

She threw her hands up and walked away, pacing around my room. "Give me time—"

"Tomorrow," I said. "I will show this to someone tomorrow afternoon."

"You psycho!" she shrieked. "You can't do this—"

The word hit hard. *Psycho.* I had heard it a million times, but never from her. My one friend. My eyes watered. I wanted to take it back. I wanted to agree to delete it. Maybe I could keep my friend. But I needed to like Sara Malvern.

"I can," I said quietly. "I already did. Tell your mom the truth. Or CPS. Someone. Tomorrow afternoon I'm showing it to my parents."

We faced each other across the room. Her face was brilliant red.

"You would throw away our friendship just like that?" she whispered.

A weight settled somewhere in my stomach.

But I knew how to play the Lead Ball. I could walk with my limbs turned to stone.

"If it means he stops hurting you . . . yes."

"You are going to break up my family—"

"No," I said. "He did that."

She threw her hands up and turned away, staring at the window, trembling.

"You aren't the same Sara I met, are you?"

"No," I whispered. "And thank you."

Erin said nothing. She took out her phone and called for a ride, pacing around the room. Then she headed for the front door, and I followed her slowly, watching as she put on her coat.

When she was dressed, she opened the door, and paused halfway out.

"I'll talk to her tomorrow," she said quietly. "Don't show anyone."

"I'll tell my parents if you don't. I mean it."

Her mouth opened, and then she hurried out, slamming the door behind her. She waited in the driveway alone. I watched her through the glass, waiting until she climbed into the car and drove off. Then I went back upstairs, knowing that I had just lost my one and only friend.

CHAPTER 28

NIGHT SKY

I played the Lead Ball all night. I think I was too tired for anything else. There were weights strapped to my arms and legs, and I lay there and thought about the last look that Erin gave me.

Betrayal and hate and who knows what else.

I was ruminating. That's what Dr. Ring called it. I listened to my mom and dad fight once before bed. I listened to the TV from downstairs. Despite everything, I didn't regret showing her. The sad thoughts wanted me to regret it. They tried to tell me I was a traitor. A freak. A psycho. Even Erin had said it.

But somewhere deeper, down where thoughts don't need a voice, I felt proud. And even lying there alone, I felt less lonely than usual. I wasn't trying to get away from Sara. I wasn't trying to change her back into something she probably never was. She had done something brave. I liked that.

I slept after that and didn't stir again until midmorning. It was a Saturday, so it was quiet. My dad usually slept late and watched college football, and my mom went out with friends. The weights were still there when I stood up, but I ignored them and went downstairs.

I sat down next to my dad on the couch. He looked at least half-awake.

"Morning, Princess," he murmured, sitting up.

"Morning, Daddy."

"What are you doing today?" he asked. "Going to the park?"

I smiled. "Maybe just watching some football."

"Really?" he said, rubbing his eyes and yawning. "You feeling okay?"

"Yeah."

I patted my pocket to make sure the cell phone was there. No calls or texts. Yet.

Would she do it? I hoped so.

If she didn't, I would have to show my mom and dad.

The morning passed slowly. Then lunch. We sat and watched football, and my mind was on everything else but that. I thought about group therapy, and Daniel, and James, and all the things that had happened in the last few weeks. I checked my cell phone again and again.

Nothing. Two o'clock passed. Then three.

"Come on, Star Child," I whispered. "Tell her."

At four I was getting nervous. I sent her a text message.

I will have to tell my parents if I don't hear from you. I'm sorry.

There was no reply. I stood up and went to my room. It was time to get the files ready.

I was halfway up the stairs when the phone rang.

I scrambled into my room and closed the door, jamming the phone to my ear.

"Hello?"

"Hi." It was Erin.

"Erin—"

"Just wait," she cut in.

Her voice was low and hard.

I heard voices in the background, getting louder. She was walking closer to somebody.

"Listen," Erin said.

The voices got louder. Yelling. Shouting.

"—I saw them! On her whole body! I will call right now!"

It was her mother.

"—you are not going—"

That was him.

"—the police if you do anything," her mother said. "We're leaving today—"

"No, you are not—"

"I've already made a report! You just get your story ready—"

The voices were suddenly muted again.

"Happy?" Erin asked.

I closed my eyes. She hated me. I could hear it in her voice.

"Where are you going?" I whispered.

"My grandparents in Maine. For a while. It depends what happens to my dad."

"I'm sorry—"

"Yeah," she said. "So am I."

She hung up, and I stood there for a moment. Then I sat down at my desk and took out the tenets. I could feel a Game coming on. False Alarm maybe. So instead I read them all aloud.

"Tenet number one. You are a Star Child for life—"

I was sitting on the couch again at seven that night. We had eaten dinner, and my dad and I were still watching football. There was a never-ending lineup of games. But Mom was out, and I wanted to be around someone, even if he was snoring beside me.

I was dozing off too when there was a knock at the door. It was quiet, and he didn't even stir.

Slipping off the couch, I went to the door and peeked out the window. Stunned, I pulled open the door to reveal Erin on the porch, hands jammed into her pockets, wreathed with snow.

"Hey," she said.

"Hey."

She was bundled up. Her hair was a mess. Her eyes were swollen from crying. There was a car in the driveway—her mom and her brother were in the front seats, bags piled in the back.

"They don't know it was you," Erin said. "I didn't tell them."

She glanced at them, and then stepped closer to me.

"You know . . . my brother punched him. After all that, he was the angriest of all."

I opened my mouth. I didn't know what to say. My eyes were filling with tears.

Erin sighed. "Mom asked if I wanted to say good-bye to you. We'll be gone for a while, I think. Dad wouldn't leave, so we are. And she called the cops. He is at the station now, I think."

"Erin—"

"I said no, at first. But we were driving and I changed my mind." She hesitated, and her eyes were glassy when she turned them back to me. "I'm angry at you. Like, crazy, crazy mad. And confused. I can't decide if I want to punch you or hug you. I know you cared. But I asked you not to get involved."

"I know," I said.

"It will take some time to get over this. I don't know if

proved anything. I still take my pills, I still go to group therapy, and I live by tenets instead of rules, but I realized that's a
part of *my* normal. I get to say what normal means, and that
makes it a lot easier to find.

And maybe I am a Star Child, or maybe I am just insane,
or maybe I am a blue whale. But no matter what, my name
is Sara Malvern, and it was nice to meet you. And if you feel
really lonely sometimes, then you aren't the only one.

If you ever get down, or feel alone, just remember the five
basic tenets:

1. You are a Star Child for life.

2. Star Children must always help each other.

3. Never be unkind to normal humans (unless they
deserve it).

4. Never be ashamed of being a Star Child.

5. A Star Child never gives up, even when it is really,
really hard.

They are all important, but maybe the last one most of all.

Do me one last favor before you go. Go look in your
eyes. Do you see the yellow rings around your pupils? I

that
just

out

She
have
sure
suffi
help

pacl
by r

and
to n
alm
at m
nov:
Chil

always think of a star emerging from the darkness. Maybe a supernova.

I look at my eyes now, and I remember that I am a Star Child. There is lots of darkness around me and sometimes my light takes a very long time to reach anything, but it does, and somebody somewhere might need to see that light, even if they never tell me about it.

started talking about our challenges. It was amazing. Some-where, I like to think that twelve-year-old kid was thinking: *All of that fear was worth it. All of it led to an opportunity to spread awareness and encourage others to TALK.*

Another topic was also very popular: the singular Sara Malvern. Readers loved her just as much as I did. They wanted to know more about her. She was the shining light in Daniel's story . . . but how did she become so self-confident? Was she always like that? How did she become that won-derfully bizarre, brilliant person? Lucky enough for me, that interest, and my amazing editor's encouragement, led me to tell this story.

Sara gave me the chance to go deeper. As anyone who deals with mental illness knows, a lot of disorders are inter-related. I dealt with OCD, but also general anxiety and panic disorders. Sometimes, I had three or four panic attacks a day. At times, depression reared its ugly head.

It all felt so shameful. All I wanted was to be better. To be *normal.*

Sara is the shining light in my story too. She gave me the chance to explore another very important relationship for all of us: the one with ourselves. This book is about changing that voice in our heads. It is about understanding and accept-ing everything that makes us weird and wonderful.

But Sara had help to get there, even if she was reluctant to accept it at first. We should never, ever be afraid to ask for